# THE MONTCLAIR EMERALDS
*Their eyes met . . . and a legend began*

It was at the French court that renegade
Charles de Montclair first kissed the hand of
the beautiful Angélique . . . and lost his
heart. Angélique, too, was bewitched.
Though promised in marriage to a powerful
duke, she defied the dictates of society and
eloped with her lover.

On his secluded estate they began a lifetime
of bliss. And as a symbol of his devotion,
Charles gave his bride an exquisite set of
jewelry—the four matchless Montclair
emeralds. Angélique cherished the gift,
knowing her husband's love shone from
each glittering stone.

A century later revolution rocked France,
and this noble couple's great-great-
granddaughter was forced to flee for her life.
Snatching up a few possessions in the dead
of night, she made her tortuous way to
freedom in the New World. Much as she
treasured her family's gift of love, she was
forced to sell the precious jewels, one by
one. And each carried with it the legacy of
the past into the future. . . .

**Vicki Lewis Thompson** is a transplanted Easterner who lives in Tucson, Arizona, with her husband and their two children. Vicki has always wanted to write. Indeed, at the age of eight she converted her bedroom closet into an "office" and spent hours curled up inside, creating poetry and stories. Before becoming a full-time author, she taught English and worked as a newspaper reporter. But now, more than eighteen romances later, she has found her niche as a romance writer, delighting her many readers with tender, warmhearted, sensual love stories.

## Books by Vicki Lewis Thompson

### HARLEQUIN TEMPTATION

Don't miss any of our special offers. Write to us at the following address for information on our newest releases.

Harlequin Reader Service
901 Fuhrmann Blvd., P.O. Box 1397, Buffalo, NY 14240
Canadian address: P.O. Box 603,
Fort Erie, Ont. L2A 5X3

# Impulse
## VICKI LEWIS THOMPSON

# *Harlequin Books*

TORONTO • NEW YORK • LONDON
AMSTERDAM • PARIS • SYDNEY • HAMBURG
STOCKHOLM • ATHENS • TOKYO • MILAN

To Richard and Sandra Griggs,
who answered my endless questions
about farm life with good humor
and tolerance.

Published September 1988

ISBN 0-373-25317-6

## 1

THE "WILLIAM TELL OVERTURE" blared from the speakers inside the henhouse as April wielded her paintbrush in the early-morning light. She didn't realize Ida Mae Lowdermilk was standing at the bottom of the extension ladder until her old friend resorted to her hog-calling voice to override the music.

"Lavender?" Ida Mae shouted. "You're painting the henhouse lavender?"

"This side," April called down without pausing in her work. She'd known Ida Mae since third grade, and they didn't stand on formalities with each other. "The rest will be apple green, daffodil and robin's-egg blue, in that order."

"I don't know if Booneville is ready for this." Ida Mae sidestepped a large glob of paint that plopped to the ground and lay like an iris petal in the dust. "Couldn't you at least stick with one color?"

"Not with the cans on sale at Bender's Hardware," April shouted back. "Besides, Irene would have loved the effect of it." She continued sweeping the brush across the weathered boards.

"Maybe she would have, God rest her soul," Ida Mae conceded, "but what will your folks think of such a thing?"

"They told me the place was mine to do with as I wanted, provided I kept the money coming in." April moved down a rung and slapped another lavender swath across the henhouse. The fresh paint smelled like beginnings, not endings, and that suited April just fine. Irene would have wanted her to look ahead, not back.

"Your music's invigorating this morning."

"The chickens asked me to turn it up. They're feeling funky today."

"I hate to think what kind of eggs they're laying with this racket. Listen, I'm getting a stiff neck and laryngitis from our conversation," Ida Mae said. "Suppose you could come down?"

"I suppose." April hung the paint bucket on the ladder and laid the brush across the top. Slowly she descended the ladder and faced Ida Mae. Her childhood friend looked the way she always did—pert and scrubbed, blond hair short and disciplined, checked blouse tucked neatly into her jeans. "Where'd you stash the kids?"

"My mother's. I thought you'd be a little upset today, and I didn't want my three little potato bugs adding to your problems."

"You could have brought them, Idie. Children would be nice to have around this morning." April realized her glasses were speckled with lavender paint, and she shoved them on top of her head. Better to have the fall landscape blurred than polka-dotted.

Ida Mae assessed April's appearance with a glance. "You look terrible."

"These are my painting clothes."

"That's not what I mean, and you know it. Your hair looks as if you tied it in a knot, and your eyes are like two burned holes in a blanket."

April shrugged. "So?"

"So come inside and I'll fix you a cup of tea." Ida Mae put an arm around April's waist and guided her toward the white farmhouse. "I guess even I didn't realize how much you loved that old woman. You're taking it mighty hard, aren't you?"

"I'm okay." April felt the tears threaten again. How stupid. She wasn't even related to Irene, although she had come close to being a granddaughter-in-law, if there was such a thing. "Mom spent the day here yesterday. She arrived soon after the news was out. She would have slept here last night, too, but I made her go home. I'm a big girl, after all."

"Who's lost a dear friend," Ida Mae added.

"I miss her already," April confessed as she walked with Ida Mae up the wooden steps and through the squeaking screen door. "I think she knew this was about to happen. She'd drop little hints, trying to prepare me. But I wouldn't pay attention, didn't want to pay attention."

"I know, I know," Ida Mae crooned.

"She had such a spark, such a neat way of looking at life. She would have been at home anywhere in the world— Paris, London, New York...."

"But she stayed right here in Booneville." Ida Mae bustled around the kitchen making a pot of tea on the old enameled stove. "That should make us all feel good about our hometown."

"Yeah, that's something she taught me, all right—to appreciate this place." April sank down on a kitchen chair and let Ida Mae fuss over her. Her friend was good at caretaking, and at the moment April was grateful that she didn't have to put up a front for this person she'd known for eighteen years.

Ida Mae set cups and napkins in front of them. "Prettiest little town in all of central Illinois, if you ask me."

"I don't know about that, Idie. But we've made progress with the square."

"We have." Ida Mae poured the tea. "I noticed today that the frost has nipped the mums a little, but they're still blooming."

"And painting the gazebo sure helped. Remember how Irene got out there and worked right along with the rest of us, as if the summer heat were only a minor nuisance? We were all drenched in sweat, and she kept whistling and painting."

"After seeing your henhouse, I'm surprised we ended up with white for the gazebo."

"Irene and I considered other colors, but we decided the sculpture, when we finally got it, would be change enough for everyone. Damn! I wish Irene had stuck around long enough to get that sculpture project through. I don't know how we'll manage without her. I kept asking her how we'd raise the money to commission an artist, but she kept telling me not to worry. Now what are we supposed to do?"

Ida Mae poured the tea and sat down. "You sound a little put out."

"Maybe I am. Irene left us in the lurch."

"But the beautification committee was your idea, April. You can continue without Irene."

"I don't have her clout in Booneville. Who will listen to me?"

"I will, and so will the others on the committee."

"That's not exactly the whole town, Idie."

"No, but don't forget Mabel's married to the president of the bank."

"Yeah." April's laugh contained no humor. "Can't you just see Henry Goodpasture loaning us money for a sculpture?" The warm tea soothed her throat, easing the lump that had stuck there ever since yesterday morning when she'd heard about Irene. "I guess the sculpture isn't so important."

"Of course it is! Stop talking like that. Irene wouldn't have tolerated a hangdog attitude from you, April Marie, so stop it this minute! Where's your hairbrush?"

April lifted an eyebrow. "Going to give me a paddling, Idie?"

"That's a thought, but I had in mind straightening out that mane of yours." She got up and walked to the back bedroom. "Never mind. I'll find it."

April gazed after her friend, bemused by the offer to brush her hair. Was she really such a wreck? Maybe so, in contrast to Ida Mae. But Idie always looked perfect, even when she was slopping hogs or riding a tractor.

"Here we go." Ida Mae stood behind April's chair and began to work. "You *did* tie this in a knot! All this beautiful chestnut hair, and you treat it like dead cornstalks."

"It's plain old brown hair, Idie. Heroines in novels have chestnut hair. Mine's brown."

"Have it your way. But you shouldn't tie it in knots."

"Couldn't find any rubber bands this morning."

"Sake's alive, woman." Ida Mae untangled the strands of hair and reached for the glasses on top of April's head. "Here, hold these."

As Ida Mae stroked the brush across April's scalp and down to her shoulders in an efficient rhythm, April began to relax. "Remember when we used to spend all night doing each other's hair and gossiping about boys, Idie?"

"I gossiped about boys, plural. You only had eyes for Dan."

April was silent for a moment. "Is he in town yet?"

"Yes. The will was read this morning, and although I don't know all that was in it, I drove out here this morning to tell you the most interesting part."

April sat up straighter in her chair. A will. April would have liked hearing it, those last requests of Irene's. But of course April wasn't privileged to hear the will because she wasn't part of Irene's family. To accomplish that she would have had to marry Dan. "And what's so interesting?" April prompted. Ida Mae loved to withhold dramatic information until the last possible moment.

"There's not going to be a funeral."

April twisted around to look at Ida Mae. "What do you mean, no funeral?"

"There'll be a private grave-side service for the immediate family, and I guess that's only Dan and his mother."

"That's all." April thought again that if she had married Dan, she would have been part of the immediate family and allowed to stand next to the grave with Dan and his mother. But she'd married wild Jimmy Foster, to everyone's dismay and eventually to her own.

"Anyway, after the burial the whole town is invited to a giant hot-dog roast on the square, all paid for by Irene. It's in the will."

"A hot-dog roast?" Gradually the confused frown cleared from April's brow, and she began to laugh. "A hot-dog roast?"

Ida Mae nodded. "With entertainment by the Booneville High School Marching Band, in uniform."

April pounded on the back of her chair with delight. "I knew she wouldn't go out just like everyone else! I knew it!"

DAN BUTLER WANDERED through his grandmother's house, touching all the things that she'd loved—shelves of books on every imaginable subject, her favorite armchair, the herb garden on the kitchen windowsill, her upright piano. He and his mother would choose the few things that they wanted, and the rest would be sold with the house. Neither his Chicago apartment nor his mother's town home in Indianapolis could hold furniture that filled a two-story house.

He tried not to think of strangers living here. Why did people have to die? Why couldn't things stay the same? Many years ago, when his father had been killed and Dan had moved into this house with his mother, he'd asked the same questions. Today he had adult logic to guide him, but he discovered logic didn't ease the pain of losing someone you loved.

"Dan."

He looked up at his mother, who stood at the head of the stairs. "I was hoping you could take a nap, Mom. Has my prowling around kept you awake?"

"No." She shook her head, and her soft blond hair ruffled with the movement. "I've been lying up there in your old bedroom thinking about you."

"Me? Why?"

His mother came down the stairs slowly. Both of them had been moving slowly the past few days, as if their hurt were physical rather than mental and quickness would sharpen the pain. "Because you're alone," she said, coming to the foot of the stairs and laying her hand on his arm. "That's not right."

"I'm not alone. I have friends. I date. I came damn close to getting married last year."

"That's just it. You've come close, but you always back away. For some reason there's no . . . magic."

"Mom, for crying out loud. Magic is for kids. I'm fast approaching thirty."

His mother shook her head again. "Magic is not just for kids. Your father and I had it."

Dan covered his mother's hand with his own and felt the familiar outlines of her heirloom ring, the one his father had given her, the same one his grandmother had received from his grandfather. "I guess you and Dad were lucky."

"Yes, we were, in spite of what happened. I know you think I'm crazy, but I believe some of our luck had to do with this ring." She pulled her hand from under his and slipped the ring from her finger. "I'm giving it to you."

"Hey." Dan stepped back and shook his head. "There's no way I'll take that from you. We may have talked about my giving it to my fiancée, but I don't have one. Even if I did, I've decided that you should keep the ring. It reminds you of Dad."

"These days it reminds me that you haven't found that special love you need. Maybe if you have the ring, something magic will happen for you."

"That's crazy."

"Dan, Irene expected this ring to be passed down. Now that she's gone, I feel a great responsibility to do so. Please take it. Humor me. Knowing that you have the ring fills me with hope for the future, and I need that right now, with so much sadness around us."

Dan hesitated a moment longer before taking the emerald-and-diamond heirloom from her outstretched palm. "This doesn't feel right."

"It will, Dan. Give it time."

ON THE DAY of the funeral and hot-dog roast the air was as crisp as a fresh apple. The streets of Booneville were lined with the vehicles of those who, like April, lived too far from town to walk. April struggled to find a parking space near the square and finally ended up two blocks away. As she got out of her pickup truck, she could hear the band strike up its fight song. April smiled. Irene had been exactly right in her plans. "The Booneville High Fight

Song" was far more appropriate for Irene than a funeral dirge.

The leaves on the giant oaks lining the town square had turned the color of butter, and the red maples beside the gazebo blushed from the first cold caress of fall. The vivid red was repeated in the band uniforms and the yards of crepe-paper streamers twirled around the gazebo posts in barber-pole fashion. April thought how much Irene would have appreciated the whole display.

The aroma of hot dogs drifted from the immense barbecue grill that had been brought over from the Baptist Church, and April decided that the Methodists and Presbyterians had emptied their church basements to provide enough long tables and folding chairs. The square was jammed with adults and children, and April wondered if any of Booneville's 1,042 residents had stayed home.

She'd intended to wait awhile before searching the crowd for Dan, but instead, her gaze went directly to him as if she had no free will. Besides, he did stand out, she argued with herself. His navy-blue suit in this year's style marked his transformation into a city boy, despite his rural roots. His dark hair showed the deft hand of a stylist instead of the utilitarian clippers used by Jake, the local barber. And Dan's face wasn't harvest-season tan as were the faces of his old high-school buddies who surrounded him.

April hated to admit what she was really looking for and dreading to find—a woman by his side, a Chicago woman with obvious claims to him. After April and Irene had become friends, Irene had confided that Dan had been involved in two serious relationships, neither of which had progressed to the engagement stage. The last thing April had heard, however, was that Dan's mother still wore the heirloom ring that had been her token of engagement and would serve the same purpose when Dan chose a bride. At one time April thought the ring might belong to her, but those days were over.

At the moment Dan appeared to be flanked only by Booneville people. If he'd brought a woman down from Chicago with him, April would know it soon enough. Anyone from the city would stand out, just as he did, and most of the people milling around on the square would be discussing Dan's new girlfriend within minutes of her arrival.

April decided to mingle and tackle the problem of speaking to Dan later. Now that Irene was gone, common decency dictated that April seek him out and express her condolences. She wished now that she hadn't avoided him quite so carefully all these years. If they had bridged the painful gap of their estrangement earlier and fallen into distant friendship, her contact with him today would have been easier.

Instead, her palms were clammy with sweat after only this brief glimpse of him. April feared that her emotional attachment to Dan still existed, but she doubted seriously that he felt the same. Not after what she'd done.

April found her mother and father in the line of people waiting for food. "May I cut in?" she teased, jostling herself between them.

"Why, the nerve of some people," her mother said with a smile. Then she turned and hugged her daughter. "You're looking much better."

April's father put his hand on her shoulder. "I'm sorry about this, honey. You were closer to Irene than most."

"I'll miss her, that's for sure."

"But you're not wearing your heart on your sleeve today," her mother said approvingly. "I like that new fall coat, and I think gold is definitely your color. Makes your eyes look like brown velvet. Especially with your contacts in instead of the glasses."

"My goodness, Mom."

"Can't I be proud of my only child?"

"But you're embarrassing me." She looked around for something to divert attention from herself. "Not everybody could give up the idea of wearing black, I see."

"Tradition dies hard, sweetheart. I reached for my black church dress three times before I finally grabbed this orange one and put it on. A lot of people are shocked by the way Irene wanted things. They expected a viewing last night at the funeral home, but of course there was none of that. I think we will have a prayer in a little bit, though. I saw Henry Goodpasture rigging a microphone up at the gazebo. By the way, have you seen Dan yet?"

"Sort of."

"I just commented to your father that Dan's even more handsome now than he was as a boy, isn't he, Pete?"

April's father snorted. "Thelma Jane, you have the subtlety of a sledgehammer."

"April knows what I mean."

"Yes, Mom, I'm afraid I do. I'm sure Dan is no longer interested in me, and unless he's changed a lot, I'm not interested in Dan."

"People forgive other people, April. Jimmy Foster was a youthful mistake on your part. Dan's a big enough person to understand that."

"Mom, please don't try to play matchmaker, okay? Irene used to drop hints all the time, too, and that was one thing about her that irritated me. Dan has known for two years that Jimmy and I were divorced, and I haven't noticed him hightailing it down from Chicago to throw himself at my feet, have you?"

"Well, he'd need some indication from you that—"

"Enough, Mom. I broke up with Dan eight years ago for a reason, and I have no proof that he's changed. The fact that he hasn't risked contacting me proves that he hasn't—that he's still careful, practical, unromantic Dan. Lovely to look at, but boring to hold."

"April!"

"Sorry, but it's the truth." Well, almost, April amended to herself. The steamy scenes in the back of Dan's Chevy still created a remembered zing of sexual excitement, even after all these years. Then there was the night of the senior prom, when Dan had driven up from Blackburn College so he could be her date.

She'd bragged to all her friends that Dan would certainly propose that night and slip the heirloom ring on her finger. Instead, he'd made his stuffy speech about waiting until he'd finished college and had a good job before they became "involved."

April had understood that his attitude was reasonable. That was the trouble. She had wanted him to love her beyond all reason, to need her so much that nothing else mattered except being together. She'd told him—cruelly—that she might not be able to wait that long. A month later she was married to Jimmy.

"April, honey, you're holding up the line." Her father's gentle nudge brought her back to the present.

Ahead of her, her mother was filling her plate and exclaiming over the variety of salads weighing down the table.

April tried to take an interest, although food was at the bottom of her priorities. "This potato salad looks like yours, Mom," she said, putting a spoonful on her plate.

"It is."

"But I thought everything was to be provided."

"It was, but we all knew that Jesse's Café wasn't up to this kind of order. Besides, most of the women wanted to bring something. We always do, when someone passes on. The family can take home the leftovers."

"I hate to say this, but I can't picture Dan loading food into his car for the drive back to Chicago, and his mother certainly won't drag it back to Indianapolis, either."

"They might decide to stay a few days, and they'll have to eat, won't they?"

April knew there was no arguing with her mother on this topic. The need to bring food for a grieving family was completely ingrained, even if the gesture was sometimes inappropriate. April hoped the townspeople would eat every last morsel so that Dan and his mother wouldn't have to deal with three-bean salad and coleslaw at the end of the day.

Across the square, Dan took advantage of a few moments alone to scan the crowd for April. He finally saw her wandering through the serving line and putting very little on her plate. He felt a tug at his heart. She didn't feel like eating, either. Perhaps she, more than anyone else here, was experiencing the same sense of desolation that his grandmother's death gave him.

An older couple came up to offer condolences, and Dan acknowledged their sympathy with half his attention as he strained to keep track of April in the crowd. The gold of her coat beckoned to him like a nugget winking from a streambed filled with more ordinary stones. The coat was belted, showing off the small waist he probably could span with his hands, even now.

He realized that all the women he'd dated in the past eight years had looked a lot like her—slim build, long legs, brown hair that shone like burnished wood in the sunshine. He'd been to bed with two and almost married one, but that had ended when he'd called her April in the midst of a passionate moment. He thought of all the times since April's divorce that his grandmother had urged him to contact his former love, but pride and the fear of a second rejection had stood in his way.

Now, in death, his grandmother had found a way around his reluctance, had managed to have the last word on whether or not he'd see April again. The terms of the will guaranteed that he and April would work together, unless she declined the board appointment. Knowing April, Dan didn't expect that. His mouth was dry at the prospect of talking to her again, and his grief made him feel exposed and vulnerable. He wanted somebody to hold, but that person couldn't be April, not so soon, anyway, and maybe not ever.

For some reason he thought of the ring tucked into the breast pocket of his suit. Ever since his mother had given it to him, he'd worried about losing it, and carrying the heirloom around in his pocket seemed the safest course. He'd forgotten that he had it there until now, when he caught sight of April. Briefly he recalled his mother's speech about the ring's magic and then dismissed her words as sentimental nonsense. Thinking of April and then the ring was just a coincidence.

Gerald Sloan, his grandmother's lawyer, appeared at his elbow with a plateful of food. "I stood in a long line to get this for you, so you'd better eat it," he said.

Dan looked at the heaped plate and shook his head. "Sorry, Gerry. You eat it."

"Hey, son, your grandmother wouldn't want you to waste away. She'd want you to take advantage of this spread."

"Did she put that in the will, too? That her grandson is required to consume so many hot dogs and so much potato salad at this crazy party?"

"Maybe she did, at that."

"Come on, Gerry. Give me a break."

"Okay. Will it bother you if I eat, then?"

"I wish you would. Maybe if your mouth's full, you'll stop hounding me about my nutrition. You sound just like Grandma. Nag, nag, nag."

"And you loved her for it."

"Yeah, Gerry, I did."

"How's your mom doing?"

"Pretty well, I think. She once told me that losing my dad was so awful that anything else that happened in her life would be duck soup in comparison."

"That's probably true. They were so much in love it was kind of like a storybook romance. Of course, some say that ring had an effect on their devotion, but I don't believe that kind of superstition."

"The way Grandma used to tell it, their relationship changed the day he gave her that ring, but I find that theory hard to believe, too. Sure, it's a valuable piece of jewelry, but so are most engagement rings."

Gerry shrugged. "Who can say? Although there *is* something about this one, maybe because of its age. It seems to have a timeless quality."

"Getting pretty philosophical, aren't you?" Dan considered telling the lawyer that the ring was now in his pocket but decided not to. Gerry would speculate about why, and Dan would have to admit that his mother was trying to marry him off.

"Yeah, well . . . I'll blame my philosophical thoughts on your grandmother." Gerry finished the food on his plate. "Speaking of that fine lady, I think we ought to make the announcement before people start heading home. Wouldn't want anyone to miss the big news."

"I guess you're right. Most everyone seems to have gotten their meal."

"Then I'll head on up to the microphone. Each of the ministers has asked to say a little prayer first. Considering that Irene liked to rotate her attendance, they all appear to have some claim on her."

Dan smiled. "And nobody has an exclusive claim. She used to drive them all crazy, playing musical churches, with me trailing right along behind her. I swear if there had been a Buddhist temple in Booneville, she'd have gone there, too."

Gerry chuckled. "No doubt. Well, I'm off. When did you say the first board meeting should be?"

"I can make it down by ten next Saturday morning."

"Fine. Chin up."

"I'm trying."

April had stood about ten feet away and out of Dan's peripheral vision while she waited for him to finish talking with Irene's lawyer. She didn't want her first conversation with Dan in eight years to be an interruption of someone else's discourse. When Gerald Sloan left, April stepped forward so that Dan could see her coming. She noticed the widening of his pupils; he was caught off guard, ill-prepared for her unexpected appearance.

She held out her hand. "I'm sorry about your grandmother, Dan." She sounded much calmer than she felt.

"I'm sorry, too, April." He took her hand and held it for a moment as he looked into her eyes. "How have you been?"

Instantly April regretted offering to shake hands with him. His firm grip was too familiar, even after all the years since she'd felt the texture of his skin. "Fine," she mumbled, aware of each of his fingers, of the creases in his palm.

She wanted to jerk her hand back as if from a hot stove, but that would give away too much. It was incredible how his touch brought back all the longing and unsatisfied passion of those nights they'd spent parked on lonely farm roads. They hadn't made love, not quite, and April remembered only too well that Dan had always been the one to call a halt. Practical Dan. She extricated her hand as gracefully as possible.

They stood for a moment in silence before he spoke. "I, uh, heard about the divorce," he said at last.

"Yes, well..." April couldn't look into the blue of his eyes any longer for fear she'd find accusations there. "Jimmy wasn't cut out for running a chicken farm, I'm afraid."

"I hear you're doing quite well, though."

"I make ends meet."

"That's saying a lot these days, with farmers declaring bankruptcy right and left." He shook his head. "I don't know why anyone would want to farm these days."

"It's an independent life, for one thing." April remembered this argument. They'd had it before. She'd always suspected Dan's aversion to farming had a lot to do with his father's death. Dan knew that farming could kill someone you loved. A tractor going up an embankment could tip over and crush the life from a man before anyone realized he was late coming home from the fields. Such a death had the power to change a little boy's life forever.

"Sure, you've got independence," Dan countered. "You're free to put in a crop and pray for the right amount of rain at the right time. If you're lucky, you harvest something, and if you're a real miracle worker, you sell your product for a decent price. That's a hell of a way to live, if you ask me."

"I suppose. I happen to like it."

"You've always been a risk-taker."

April searched for any malice in his tone and could find none. "Thank you," she said, deciding to accept his statement as a compliment.

"Besides, your farm is diversified, with the beehives and the pick-your-own produce to supplement the eggs you sell." He grinned. "I've heard you've renamed the place, too."

"Corny, huh? Ida Mae suggested it as a joke, and I decided it might bring in more business."

"I bet it does. But how many people show up expecting lectures on sex? If I saw a sign advertising The Birds and the Bees, that's what I'd think."

April laughed. "That's because you've always had your mind on—" She stopped and glanced up quickly into his eyes. The old spark was there, and the sexual excitement was zinging between them as if eight years hadn't come and gone. April was aghast that the attraction could bloom again so fast. She cleared her throat. "But I'll admit farming's still chancy, compared to your job. How do you like the big city?" she asked more formally.

He took his cue from her tone. "Lake Michigan's nice. Business is good."

"But do you like it?"

"Chicago's very noisy, April. The sirens get to me the most, but . . ." He sighed. "Yeah, I like it okay."

"Dan, you don't sound—"

Static from the loudspeakers interrupted their discussion, and Dan laid a hand automatically on her arm. "Listen, April. Perhaps I should warn you about something."

"Let us pray," boomed a voice from the speakers.

Dan dropped his hand from her arm, and they both ducked their heads obediently. The prayers offered were for a woman they both loved, and they concentrated on the comforting words with a closeness of spirit they hadn't known for many years.

When April heard a choked sound from Dan, she knew he was fighting to keep from giving way to his emotions, and she reached out and laced her fingers through his. He gripped her hand tightly until the last of the solemn prayers was over, and then with a shaky sigh he released his pressure on her fingers. She didn't look at him. Her eyes were brimming, and she was certain his were, too. He wouldn't want her to notice.

At the end of the prayers for Irene, Gerald Sloan went up to the microphone and adjusted it for his shorter height. He took a piece of paper from his coat pocket, as if he'd written a small speech.

The lawyer cleared his throat. "Citizens of Booneville, your late friend and neighbor, Irene Butler, greets you. She hopes you had a wonderful time this afternoon, and that this celebration will serve as a model to improve other such usually dreary occasions."

April leaned over to whisper to Dan. "I bet she wrote that!"

"Yep, she did."

Gerald Sloan continued to read. "Most of you know me as a simple country woman, which I am, but I've been able, through investments, to amass an embarrassingly large estate. I hereby bequeath the income of the estate, which will amount to approximately two hundred and fifty thousand dollars a year, to the town of Booneville."

April gasped.

"The distribution of the money will be supervised by my grandson, Daniel Butler, with the aid of a board of directors that I have personally selected from the townspeople. Those directors, if they are willing to serve, will be Henry Goodpasture, Gerald Sloan, M.G. Tucker, Bill Lowdermilk and April Foster."

April's mouth dropped open, and she looked at Dan in bewilderment. Irene had put her on the board with all those men? And with Dan?

He answered her unspoken questions with an uneasy smile. "You know, April, she always did like to make things interesting."

# 2

APRIL STOOD IN A DAZE as Gerry Sloan finished his speech with the information that the first board meeting would be the following Saturday, and anyone unable to serve on the board should contact him immediately.

"Will you do it?" Dan asked gently.

"I...I don't know. I guess so. That's what she wanted." Gradually April recovered her equilibrium. "How long have you known about this?"

"Just since the reading of her will. I had no idea she had so much money. Nobody did."

"But you could have been rich," April said, blurting out the first thing that came to her mind. Then she blushed at having spoken aloud a truth that must be embarrassing to Dan.

Dan didn't seem embarrassed. "She wouldn't plunk two million dollars down and say, 'Here, Dan.' That wasn't her style. She wants me to earn my money, just as she earned hers. You should know that, as close as you were to her."

"We couldn't have been too close, for her to have two million dollars I didn't know about."

"But, April, nobody knew, not until Gerald Sloan opened the safe-deposit box and found all the deeds and stock certificates."

"I still can't believe it. If she was a millionaire, why did she drive that old Plymouth? Why did she buy paper napkins on sale, like the rest of us? She could have afforded linen ones and thrown them away after each meal!"

"And what if she had? Would your relationship with her have been exactly the same?"

April paused to consider his question. It was an interesting thought. She started to answer just as the high-school band launched into a spirited version of "Stars and Stripes Forever."

Dan leaned closer to her. "Could we go somewhere and talk?"

"I don't think so," April said, glancing behind him. "Here comes Henry Goodpasture bringing half the town to express their gratitude, no doubt."

"Damn. There are some things that we—"

"Later," April murmured as Henry came up and placed a fatherly arm around Dan's shoulders. Following close behind were various townspeople, including the Lowder-milk clan, Ida Mae among them.

"I'm bowled over," Henry said. "Just bowled over by all this, Daniel."

"I was a little surprised myself when I heard the will read on Wednesday, Mr. Goodpasture."

"Call me Henry, son." The banker smoothed his mustache. "After all, we'll be working together now to manage this generous bequest of your grandmother's. I can see it now...." And he swept one arm toward the horizon to indicate the scope of his dreams.

April looked away, unable to deal with Henry's grandiose gestures. He'd always been far too officious for her tastes.

"First we can repave a few streets," Henry proclaimed royally, as if everyone would naturally accord him command of the projects. "Then we'll fix the 4-H building's roof, maybe even get a *new* 4-H building. And then the streetlights are looking pitiful. We could use some better ones out on Terrell Road. And we can't forget the cemetery. That fence around the perimeter is practically falling down thanks to termites."

Ida Mae touched April's elbow. "Come on over here a minute," she said close to April's ear.

April turned with relief from Henry's dissertation and followed Ida Mae to a spot away from the crowd gathering around Dan.

"Can you *believe* this?" Ida Mae exclaimed.

"Not really." April shook her head. "Two million smackers. Whew!"

"All that time she struggled along with us while we ran bake sales and bazaars for the beautification committee, and she could have ended our misery with one stroke of her pen. Why, April?"

"I asked Dan the same thing, and he asked if we'd have treated her the same way, if we'd known."

"Maybe we'd have treated her better!"

"I think that's what he meant, Idie. She wouldn't have been one of us anymore. Her wealth would have set her apart from the simple joys we all share in Booneville."

"You mean the simple joys of struggling through a winter because the price of hogs went down again? Or repairing a tractor so many times that you think you could have built your own more easily? To think that whenever I complained to her about our problems, I imagined she understood."

"She did, Idie. Don't be hard on her. I'm beginning to see why she kept quiet about her investments, although I admit the news was pretty shocking at first."

"Why did she do it, if she wasn't planning to tell anyone or spend the money?"

April thought for a moment. "Maybe for the challenge. She loved an interesting challenge."

"That's true. Maybe you're right. Well, at least you'll get your sculpture now."

"My sculpture?" April stared at her in confusion. "Why would you think that?"

"You're on the board that will decide where this money goes, so just allot some for the sculpture you wanted. And make it expensive."

"I doubt I'd get it approved." April glanced at the knot of people surrounding Dan, with Henry Goodpasture still holding court concerning all the wonderful projects he had in mind. "Did you hear what Henry was talking about? He's interested in roads and roofs and streetlights, all very practical things. I'm only one board member, and the only woman at that. What chance will I have of wangling money for a piece of sculpture? Henry's already assuming leadership, as he usually does."

"You've got a good chance. I'll get Bill to vote for it, and M.G. can be persuaded, I'll bet. Irene always liked him. And then there's Dan."

"Yes, and then there's Dan." She gazed across at his strong profile as he waited for Henry to run down.

"After what you two once were to each other, I can't believe he wouldn't go along with your ideas about the sculpture."

"Oh, I can, Idie." April thought about the night of the prom, when she'd expected moonlight and extravagant promises of love everlasting. Instead, she'd got a speech that even included statistics about how few married students finish college. "I can believe that Dan would think something like a sculpture would be a complete waste of his grandmother's money."

"But you'll try, won't you? You will serve on the board, I hope."

"Yes, I'll serve on the board. It's the least I can do for Irene."

"You know why she named you, April. She knew the men wouldn't have the imagination to appropriate money for things like artwork and other so-called 'useless' projects. She's counting on you to fight for beauty, as well as practicality."

"Maybe." April looked over at Dan. What Ida Mae had said made sense, but April couldn't shake the thought that Irene had been up to something far more personal when she put April on the board with Dan. April wondered if Dan suspected it, too. "Well, Idie, I need to pay my respects to Dan's mother, although I kind of dread seeing her. She's not terribly fond of me."

"That was a long time ago. Don't worry about it. She must still be friends with your folks, at any rate. I saw her talking to them over by the barbecue grill."

"I wouldn't expect her to blame them for the actions of their daughter. But I'm a different story."

Ida Mae gazed at her friend. "How do you feel, now that you've talked to him again?"

"Oh, I don't know." April didn't have to ask which "him" Ida Mae meant. "It's hard to tell about a person in a few short minutes after you haven't seen him for eight years." April wasn't quite ready to confess the disturbing heat that had invaded her when Dan's hand closed around hers. "I imagine he's the same old Dan."

"Now that you're on this board, you should be able to tell soon enough. I'll say this—he hasn't gotten any uglier over the years."

"No," April agreed, "he hasn't." She glanced in his direction once more and found him looking at her. April turned her head away. "Where did you say his mother was?"

"Over by the barbecue grill," Ida Mae replied patiently.

"Ida Mae, get that little smile off your face. I don't plan for anything to start up again between Dan and me. Too much water has gone under the bridge."

"Of course. I was just admiring how well he's kept himself in shape."

"Uh-huh. You don't fool me, Idie."

"You don't fool me, either, April."

"I'll call you next week."

"You do that."

As she walked away from Ida Mae, April sighed. One drawback, or maybe an advantage, of knowing someone forever was being transparent to them. She wouldn't be able to fool Ida Mae into thinking she no longer cared about Dan Butler.

Well, shoot, she'd always cared about him. Just because you cared about someone didn't mean everything was hunky-dory between the two of you, April thought morosely. She wondered if there was any chance that Dan had become more impulsive and creative in his approach to life. Or was he still the careful boy who had smashed her dreams? His reaction to her sculpture project would reveal a lot. Once again April considered how much of this little drama Irene had envisioned when she drew up the terms of her will.

April spotted her parents and Dan's mother exactly where Ida Mae had indicated they would be. April had always had trouble imagining that Dan and this woman were related. Dan's large, athletic build and dark hair must be an echo of his late father rather than the slight blond person who had given birth to him.

April's mother waved as April drew near. "Here she is, now. We were just discussing how well both of our children are doing, weren't we, Jeanne?"

"Yes, we were. How are you, April?"

"Okay, considering." April remembered as she gazed at Jeanne Butler that mother and son shared one trait: they both had the same deep blue eyes. Jeanne's were fringed with blond lashes, however, and Dan's with black. Jeanne didn't use mascara, and the result was a look of vulnerability, made more poignant by her tragic story of lost love. Today those vulnerable eyes, dull from weeping, gave April an idea of how much Jeanne grieved for the loss of another loved one.

"I understand you've made a success with the farm," the blond woman continued.

April suspected that Dan's mother hadn't forgotten that this was the person who had broken her son's heart, but she was trying to be gracious under the circumstances. April had to admire her for that effort. "Did they tell you about the new name and painting the henhouse?"

Dan's mother smiled. "Oh, I heard about that soon after I hit town. Everyone's gotten quite a kick out of your innovations. I told your parents that they reminded me of things Irene would have done."

April was pleased. "She thought The Birds and the Bees was a little cutesy, but she was all in favor of the painting project. I've been threatening to do it for months."

"How did you ever think of such an idea?"

"It's not original. When I was in Canada with—" She stopped herself before saying "with Jimmy." "When I traveled through the Canadian Maritimes, I noticed the farm buildings were often painted wild colors, although not necessarily several on one building. That was my embellishment after I discovered a paint sale at Bender's.

Anyway, Irene liked my plan of bringing a touch of Canada here. I wish she could have seen my henhouse."

"So do I." Jeanne's blue eyes grew more friendly. "I owe her a great deal. Did you know that she paid for my secretarial training?"

April shook her head.

"I tried to repay her later, but she wouldn't hear of it."

Jeanne gestured as she talked, and April watched her intently. Something was different about this woman, April thought. Something was missing. What was it?

"After I got that great job offer in Indianapolis," Dan's mother continued, "when Dan was fifteen and balked at leaving Booneville High—" At this point Jeanne paused and looked pointedly at April. Everyone in the little circle knew that April had been one of the main reasons Dan protested the move to Indianapolis.

April smiled in a self-deprecating way. She'd been only thirteen when Dan made his rebellious stand. She'd foolishly expected him to continue making such dramatic gestures on her behalf. Only later had she realized that leaving Booneville right before his junior year must have seemed riskier to Dan than staying, despite his mother's absence. Even without his interest in April, he wouldn't have wanted to go.

"Anyway, Irene was the one who insisted I take the job and let Dan stay with her to finish out high school. She was very wise to see how much I needed that job to get a new lease on life, and Dan had pretty much outgrown his dependence on me, anyway. He was always so responsible."

April's parents murmured their assent without looking at April. All three of them had been over this ground a million times, as her mother and father struggled to understand why Dan's sense of responsibility had driven April away from him and into the arms of a wild boy like

Jimmy Foster. April was afraid they blamed most of it on April's being an only child and willful. She hoped the reasons ran deeper than that.

Jeanne sighed. "I'm really going to miss Irene." She glanced around at the festive gathering. "This is so like her, to turn a funeral into a celebration. And to give her money to the town she loved so much."

"It's unusual, that's for sure," April's father said, glancing at Jeanne uneasily.

"I certainly wouldn't have wanted that money." Jeanne answered his unspoken concern. "I like my life the way it is. And I'm not sure I'd want Dan to suddenly come into two million dollars, either. He's dependable now, but what would that kind of wealth do to him?"

"It didn't seem to ruin Irene." April was a little impatient with Jeanne's attitude. She figured that Dan would be too conservative, if anything, with large sums of money. He might never consider an around-the-world cruise, for example, or a custom-tailored silk suit.

"Irene was one of a kind," Jeanne replied. "We'll feel her influence for a long time to come."

"I'm sure we will," April agreed as she keyed in on the movement of Jeanne's hands. Then April knew what was different about Jeanne Butler, and the knowledge made her cold with apprehension. The emerald-and-diamond heirloom ring, the valuable piece of jewelry that had graced the blond woman's left hand for as long as April could remember, was no longer there.

THE FOLLOWING WEEK was a long one for April. She couldn't seem to get her mind off the subject of Dan and the heirloom ring. She hadn't had the courage to mention the ring to Jeanne Butler, for fear the news would be bad. If Dan had given it to someone, if he had found the love of his life, April didn't want to find out from his mother, who might not be willing to spare April much pain in the telling.

Saturday was the first board meeting, and the prospect of being in close contact with Dan again so soon knotted her stomach with dread. The same sexual attraction existed between them, and yet Dan might already be planning his wedding to someone else.

The decision to marry would have had to be a recent one because Irene would have told her otherwise. Maybe he'd decided this very week. Perhaps in this time of grieving he'd reached out to someone. With one of the anchors in his life gone, he might have wished to establish another close bond. April vowed to find out somehow on Saturday so she would know exactly how things were before she and Dan had to spend any more time together.

April missed Irene with a sharpness that surprised her. She hadn't realized how often she used to pick up the phone and call Irene to discuss ideas for the square, or just to chat. Twice during the last week April had dialed the first few digits of Irene's number before she remembered that no one would answer.

Sometimes April wondered if she'd been a bother to the older woman. In the last two months Irene hadn't felt well, yet she'd never indicated to April that she lacked the energy for their frequent brainstorming sessions. April liked to think that she helped keep Irene active and interested in life, right up to the end. Irene certainly had been an inspiration for her.

On April's infrequent trips to town, she looked, out of long habit, for Irene's Plymouth in the driveway of the house on Irving Street. But of course the Plymouth had already been sold, to someone from Decatur, and the house was up for sale, as well. The proceeds would be added to the estate, thus providing even more money for the town of Booneville.

April's days were busy, as usual. She insulated the beehives against the approaching cold weather and attacked her vegetable garden with the Rototiller. In the late afternoons she supervised the crew of high-school students who picked apples from her small orchard and bagged them for sale.

Painting the henhouse had increased her egg business. People now drove out "just to see that doggone rainbow building" and bought a few dozen eggs "as long as they'd made the trip." Many also took home a jar of honey, some squash and a pumpkin or two. April anticipated her usual brisk pumpkin sales as Halloween approached.

Each evening after chores and a light supper, she sat at the kitchen table to jot down ideas for presenting the sculpture project to the board on Saturday morning. At these moments April longed for Irene's wit and wisdom all the more. April wanted her presentation to be convincing, and Irene would have known just what to say. More important, she would have known what *not* to say.

After April's vagabond days with Jimmy, in which they'd traveled through most of North America and all of Europe, she had an expanded idea of what a sculpture on the square might look like. She especially liked the free-flowing work of modern artists such as Picasso, who were content to suggest a form rather than deliberately define one.

She was aware, however, that Booneville residents might take some time getting used to such an idea. Irene had been the only member of the beautification committee who knew the type of sculpture April had in mind. Irene had thought the contrast of old and new, the Victorian gazebo versus the ultramodern piece of art, would work well. Irene also had envisioned something designed so that children might play on it, just as they played around the gazebo. April could see nothing wrong with that, either. But how much should she say about all this to conservative people such as Henry Goodpasture and Dan Butler?

By Saturday morning, as she drove her pickup truck to the bank for the meeting, a pile of scribbled notes by her side, April was a jumble of nerves. She'd worn her glasses instead of her contacts in the interest of appearing more serious-minded, and she had on a dress for the second time that month—surely a record for her.

Once she'd chosen the dress route instead of jeans, she had felt committed to go the whole nine yards, with nylons and her best brown heels. The offerings of her jewelry box were scant, but she'd unearthed some gold hoops for her ears and a gold-link bracelet that went well with her forest-green dress. Thank goodness she'd bought a new fall coat this year, she thought, parking the truck in front of the bank. Otherwise, she'd be wearing the ratty parka she'd bummed all over Europe in, and Henry Goodpasture would mentally label her a hippie when she walked in the door.

She glanced at the vehicles already lined up at the curb. She recognized them all except one, a sporty little red Honda Civic CRX. That must be Dan's car, she thought, trying to get a fix on his choice of transportation. The color wasn't conservative. Hadn't he once told her that red cars got more speeding tickets than any other color? But April also knew that Hondas were famous for good gas mileage, which sounded exactly like the old Dan. Maybe his fiancée had picked the color.

"Hey, April, ready for the first meeting?"

At the sound of Bill Lowdermilk's voice, she turned with a grateful smile. Bill was fair-haired, like his wife, but unlike her he always looked a little mussed. His face was perpetually sunburned, and his hair was beginning to thin on top. April gazed at him fondly. He was her only guaranteed friend on this board. "I don't know, Bill. I'm really nervous."

Bill put an arm around her shoulders as they walked into the bank. "Don't worry. Idie made me promise during breakfast this morning that I'd back you, no matter what crazy scheme you have."

April laughed. She could picture Ida Mae waving a spatula under Bill's nose and extracting his promise before she served him his sausage and eggs. "I really appreciate your support, Bill. But you don't want to make Henry mad. After all, he does hold the note on your farm."

"Henry doesn't scare me none," Bill drawled, lapsing into the country-boy accent he used whenever he joked around.

"Well, he scares *me*," April admitted. "Now hush, Bill, before you get us both in trouble. I assume we're meeting in the back room."

"Seeing as how nobody's out here in the lobby, I think you're right. Ready?"

"I'm a lot readier than I was before you showed up. Let's go."

They walked through the lobby toward a dark wooden door marked Private, and April's heart began to pound. Dan was on the other side of that door, and the knowledge gave her goose bumps. She also realized that showing her feelings at this point could land her in a mess, especially if Dan was engaged. As Bill opened the door for her, she composed her face into a neutral mask.

The bank's windowless conference room was nearly filled by a long heavy table surrounded by matching chairs upholstered in green leather. At April's entrance, the four men seated around one end of the table stood up. April smiled nervously at their show of manners. Being the only woman in the group wouldn't be easy.

"Please sit down," she said, unconsciously looking to Dan for help. Today he wore slacks and a blue velour pullover that echoed the color of his eyes. He looked so good that she wondered if she could keep from staring at him throughout the meeting. "Under the circumstances, I think I should be treated like any other board member."

Dan caught her pleading glance. "April's right," he said, sitting down. "We're all equals here. That was my grandmother's intent, as you'll see in a moment." He gave April and Bill a friendly smile. "Glad you're both here. It's not quite ten yet, but we may as well start. I guess everyone was eager to discuss spending money this morning."

"Money is my business," Henry said, leaning back in his chair and smoothing his mustache.

April figured the statement was meant to underline Henry's position in the group. He had no intention of being "equal" as Dan had put it, but April understood why Irene had named him to the board. Had he been overlooked, he would have caused all kinds of problems out of hurt pride. April and Irene had discussed the same situation when they formed the beautification committee and finally had included Henry's wife, Mabel, in order not to create a powerful enemy.

As for the other members of the board, Gerald Sloan's appointment wasn't surprising. If Irene had trusted him with her legal affairs, she'd trust him in this. Bill Lowdermilk had assumed a leadership position among the younger farmers in the area, so he was a logical choice, and M.G. Tucker was one of the kindest men April had ever known. She'd always wondered if his interest in Irene went beyond neighborliness, but the older woman had never openly encouraged him in all her years of widowhood.

"Before we begin discussing possible projects, I'd like to explain how my grandmother wanted this board to operate," Dan said, opening a folder in front of him and taking out some papers to pass around the table. "I've made copies of the provisions so each of you can read them, but I'd still like to talk about the structure of the group so there will be no misunderstandings."

April felt encouraged by the strength and determination in Dan's voice. For one thing, he had mastered his grief well enough to conduct this meeting with authority, and he also didn't sound ready to turn the decisions over to Henry Goodpasture.

"As you'll see by the sheet in front of you," Dan continued, "my grandmother appointed six members on purpose. Although I'll run the meetings and eventually write the checks, each of us has an equally weighted vote when it comes to project approval. That means that with an even number on the board, we could have a tie. My grandmother meant that as a test of our ability to work together. Five members would have made the decisions too easy."

"This looks like Irene's handiwork, all right," M.G. said, adjusting his wire-rimmed glasses. "She liked to keep the pot boiling."

Henry shook his head. "Almost all governing boards are uneven numbers. We could end up in a stalemate this way. Then what?"

"That's what the last paragraph is about," Dan said. "If the board ties on a vote, we have ten days to reconsider. If we are still unable to agree, all the money reverts to the state. Oh, and if all six of us can't agree to work under these conditions, the same thing will happen."

"That's ridiculous!" Henry peered at the offending paragraph.

M.G. laughed out loud. "That's Irene. In order to keep the money for Booneville, we'll have to work as a team. I think it's a beautiful plan. I agree to it."

"So do I," Bill said, tossing his copy of the provisions on the table.

Dan looked around the room. "Gerry?'

"You've got my vote."

Henry glared at the paper for another few seconds. "Mine, too, I suppose," he mumbled, "although I don't know why she couldn't have appointed five or seven of us."

At last Dan focused on April, who had been sitting silently at the end of the table. "How about you, April? Are you in?"

She stared at him, trying to make sense of Irene's provisions. Then the puzzle pieces fell into place. Irene envisioned Bill, M.G. and April as the liberal influences on the board. Henry Goodpasture and Gerald Sloan were on the conservative side of the fence. If Dan sided with them, they'd have a certain tie over issues such as her sculpture project. Irene had planned her strategy carefully.

April realized that she was expected to work with Dan, win him over to her side on the more creative projects. Irene might have hoped that in the process April and Dan would rediscover their old love. But obviously Irene hadn't counted on Dan's becoming engaged between the time she wrote her will and the first meeting of this board.

"April?" Dan said again.

She felt a stab of pain at what might have been if Irene's plan had worked. Instead, Irene may have bequeathed

April the disturbing task of working closely with Dan while she watched him marry someone else. But did she have a choice? "I'm in," she replied.

# 3

WARMTH FLICKERED in Dan's blue eyes. "Good."

April wondered how much of Irene's strategy Dan had figured out. He must have guessed that Irene wanted to throw the two of them together, but did it make any difference now? Of course, April realized that the complex structure of this endowment had many objectives other than matchmaking.

In order for the town to continue receiving its legacy, these six people would have to work in harmony. What a challenge Irene had given them on that one! Not only were April and Dan obligated to get along, but Henry Goodpasture and M.G. Tucker, a volatile combination if April ever saw one, had to, as well.

She glanced at the other two men sitting at the table. Gerald Sloan was easygoing but conservative, and Bill Lowdermilk had the liberal ideas of the younger farmers in the area. Given the makeup of the group, keeping the money in Booneville would be a small miracle, but Irene had loved working miracles.

*And so do I*, thought April, looking straight at Dan. *Let the action begin.*

As if in answer to her thoughts, Dan flipped open a steno pad and picked up a black pen. "I suggest we establish a list of projects as our first step. As you make suggestions, give an estimate as to how much money you think the work would require. Then we'll vote on which ones to do this year."

April cringed. An outstanding sculpture would cost thousands of dollars. What chance would such a request have when these men could imagine using those thousands in some less nebulous way? She decided to wait awhile before giving her suggestion.

Henry leaned forward immediately. "Streetlights," he intoned. "The best crime deterrent in the world is good lighting, which Booneville is sadly lacking. That should be number one."

"Crime?" M.G. looked amused. "What crime, Henry?"

"Just last week Hazel Fitzsimmons had a pumpkin pie stolen from her back porch, not ten minutes after she set it out to cool."

M.G. winked at April. "My, that's serious. Would a streetlight have prevented that, do you think? I thought they usually went along the street, which wouldn't do anybody's back porch much good."

"That's not the point," Henry flushed. "In fact, the pie was stolen in the afternoon. The point is that it was a pie last week, but it could be a television set next, or the cookie jar you keep your cash in, M.G.."

"Come on, Henry. You're just sore because I haven't got every penny in this bank of yours so you can fool with it."

Dan cleared his throat. "Uh, gentlemen, let's continue. How much would streetlights cost, Henry?"

Henry named an approximate figure, and Dan wrote it down. Bill spoke next, pointing out, as Henry had the week before, that the 4-H building could use a new roof and a good coat of paint. Gerald Sloan reported that the basketball court in the gym was in pathetic shape, and M.G. brought up the matter of new high-school band uniforms. Henry said they had looked fine to him last Saturday, and Dan steered them away from yet another argument.

As he wrote on the legal pad, Dan wondered if his grandmother had held some long-hidden grudge against him, to put him in charge of this mess she'd carefully concocted. These people would never get along, if the first interchange was any example. Of course, if they couldn't agree, the money would simply go to the state and his job would end. Dan glanced at April and realized he didn't want that to happen.

Part of the problem was meeting in this bank, where Henry felt comfortable and in command. Dan realized he'd accepted Henry's offer of the room last week because he'd been too muddled with grief to realize the implications of meeting here, where Henry's power over the community was so evident. Next time they'd find another spot, a more neutral gathering place. That is, they would if they met a second time.

Dan took another suggestion from Bill Lowdermilk and two more from Henry, but he was watching April, who hadn't said much of anything yet. He'd noticed the glasses when she first came in. She was doing her female version of a Clark Kent disguise again.

In high school she'd worn them, a similar large round pair, when she wanted to impress someone with her scholarly attitude. The glasses made her appear quiet and unassuming, but Dan knew better. Did he ever! April became a different sort of woman when she took off those glasses.

He felt the dull beginning ache of desire as he recalled the night she lost a contact lens during a heavy petting session in the backseat of his Chevy. They'd both been pretty worked up, but he'd decided they should turn on the overhead light to look for the damn thing, which was expensive. Afterward she'd insisted the mood was ruined and had made him take her home. She would rather have lost the contact, she said. He remembered that she'd almost lost something else that night.

Dan cleared his throat. "April, how about you? Any ideas for spending this money?"

A faint pink spread over her cheeks. Her blush, combined with the owlish glasses, made her look much younger than twenty-seven. "Yes, I do." She picked up the papers in front of her and glanced at them before folding the whole batch and shoving them to one side. "I think we need a sculpture on the town square," she announced.

Henry stared at her. "Haven't I heard something about this before? Sounds like what Mabel was gabbing about with the beautification committee you two are on together."

"Yes, we have discussed the possibility, but we had no idea how to pay for it." April met Henry's stare. "Irene Butler was on the committee, as well."

"All right," Dan said, turning to his notepad. "Let's put the sculpture on the list. How much?"

"Wait a danged minute," Henry objected. "A statue is all well and good, but what does it do for the town? Just provides an outdoor facility for pigeons, if you ask me." He leaned back and grinned at his own humor.

April noticed that Henry had used the word "statue" instead of "sculpture," but she didn't bother to correct him. If he had an image of some soldier on a horse, that was probably better than if he fully understood her intentions. "I realize all the other suggestions are important," April said, "but so is beauty. People need something to look at that will interest them, intrigue them, lift their spirits."

Gerald Sloan gave her a kindly look. "Don't you think leaky roofs and rutted streets ought to come first, April?

It's difficult to have high spirits if the rain's coming in on you."

"No, I won't fall into that trap," April replied. "If we accomplish all the practical tasks first, we'll never get around to spending money on something just because it's beautiful. I say money should be allotted to the project this year, even if some of the other things have to wait."

M.G.'s tone was placating. "I understand your enthusiasm, April, but people around here are having hard times. They might not appreciate money being spent on something with no demonstrable value."

April sat up straighter. "I disagree. A stunning piece of art on the square is exactly what Booneville needs, perhaps more than any of these other improvements, just *because* times are tough. People need to be reminded that life shouldn't be reduced to profits and losses. We're all still dreamers, aren't we?"

*You certainly still are*, Dan thought. *Oh, lady, you haven't changed at all.* "Give me a figure, April."

She closed her eyes for a moment before naming a generous amount. She heard the quick intake of breath around the table. All of them, including Bill, thought the estimate was foolishly extravagant.

"I think it's time to vote," Dan said. "Remember we've got approximately two hundred and fifty thousand to spend. I'd advise each of you to total your choices on a piece of paper before we vote. Obviously we can't do everything this year."

April sighed. If M.G. wouldn't support her, she had little chance, unless maybe Dan . . . but no, she didn't expect that. From the murmurs around the table as they prepared to vote, she knew the sculpture project wouldn't take place this year—probably not any year. It would be disregarded each time as more "worthy" ideas came up.

Dan conducted the vote democratically, she had to admit, taking projects in order of how many considered them important. Quickly the big money was decided and only a few thousand were left. Not enough for the sculpture, in April's estimation.

"Well, what about this project of April's?" M.G. asked. "I've got it on my list. Anybody else?"

"I do," Bill said.

April gave him a grateful smile. Ida Mae would hear about this. Bill was a true friend. "So do I, of course," she said.

"Me, too," Dan said.

April tried to conceal her shock, apparently without success.

"I think April's a little surprised that some of us consider culture an important element," Dan added with a lopsided smile.

"That's not true." April ducked her head and studied the sheet in front of her. "Anyway, there's not enough money left to cover my estimate for the sculpture."

"Take less," M.G. suggested.

"Less?" She studied M.G.'s face. He was telling her that this was her chance. She could have a smaller amount now, or possibly nothing in the future. April believed he'd assessed the situation well.

"All right," she said, turning to Dan. "Let's vote on this amount for the sculpture."

Dan looked around at the group. "Objections?"

"Yes." Henry leaned his forearms on the table. "Each of you should realize that if you vote this money for some statue, we won't get the new fence around the cemetery. Simple as that. Lots of us have loved ones buried in there, and we'd like to see them properly fenced in."

A muffled sound came from M.G. Then he cleared his throat. "Henry, they aren't going anywhere."

"Let's take that vote," Dan said quickly, biting down on his lower lip. "Bill?"

"In favor of the sculpture," Bill said.

April wasn't surprised that M.G. also voted for the sculpture and that Henry and Gerald voted against. When Dan voted in favor, giving her the money, she restrained her first flash of excitement. After all, if he'd voted against her, there would have been a tie. If it had held, all their work today would have been wasted. Dan's vote was practical, after all.

"So you have something, at least," M.G. said after the vote was complete.

"I hope it's enough to find a good sculptor," April replied.

"Where were you planning to look?"

"I'd hoped to tour the galleries in Chicago and find someone there."

Henry sat back, nursing his first defeat. "Chicago, huh? There's some weird stuff up there. Like that Picasso, for example. You ever seen that, Gerry?" He turned to the only person who had supported him in the negative vote.

"It's different, all right," the lawyer agreed. "What you got in mind, April?"

"Well, I—"

"Tell you what would make me feel a whole lot better about this," Henry interrupted. "Dan lives in Chicago. How about if he goes around to the galleries with April and sort of supervises?"

April bristled. "Supervises?"

"Might be a good plan," Gerry said. "More than one member of the board should be in on the choice of the artist, anyway."

"Yeah, April," Bill added. He'd looked increasingly uncomfortable after Henry's mention of the Picasso. "Why not have Dan tag along? He's got good taste."

"I'd be glad to," Dan said, pretending to ignore the rebellious jut of April's chin. "Does everyone agree on that, then?"

M.G.'s eyes twinkled. "Sure."

April clenched her hands in frustration. "But I don't need—"

"We'd all feel better about it, April," Henry said, smoothing his mustache.

April wanted to rip out that neatly trimmed mustache, hair by hair. "In that case, of course we'll do it that way," she said with a gracious smile.

"As long as we're going to have this statue," Henry continued, "I'll tell you what I think would look real good. I'd like to see old U. S. Grant in full uniform, riding his horse into battle against the Rebels. Wouldn't that be something to be proud of?"

April looked up at the ceiling to keep from laughing. In her imagination she'd predicted that Henry would suggest exactly this sort of statue. She'd figured he'd want either Grant or Abraham Lincoln.

"Grant would be nice," Gerry agreed. "Or Lincoln. Maybe Honest Abe splitting rails. That would look good in bronze. Don't you agree, April?"

"Well, actually, I think Lincoln and Grant have been a little overdone in Illinois," she began cautiously.

"But everybody knows who they are," Henry said. "You don't want to go putting up a statue of some fellow that nobody knows."

April couldn't resist. "Why does it have to be a man?"

The room was completely silent.

"Now wait a minute," Gerry said finally. "We don't want any *Venus de Milo* type thing right on the square, where the kids will play, and everything . . ." His face turned the dull red of an old barn.

April covered her mouth with her hand and bent her head. Bless their hearts, these men thought sculptures were either men doing noble deeds or naked women. Boone-ville definitely needed this work of art, which would be neither one, if she got her way.

"I'm sure April wasn't planning something like that," Dan said without much conviction.

She glanced at him. He was giving her a look of warning, and she longed to throw them all into a tizzy by suggesting that the sculpture might be of a nude woman *and* man. But she'd only be defeating her purpose by keeping them stirred up. "No, I wasn't planning anything like that," she said, and watched them all sink back with relief.

"Of course you weren't," Henry said. "Besides, Dan wouldn't go along with that sort of foolishness. He's a sensible young man, and I know we can trust him in this. When will you go to Chicago, do you think?"

April thought quickly. "Soon. Right after Halloween, perhaps, if my parents will take care of the farm for a few days." Belatedly she remembered that Dan was supposed to be a part of all this. "Of course, I can work around your schedule, Dan, if that's not convenient," she added with exaggerated courtesy. And what about his fiancée, if indeed he had one? April's presence in Chicago might be awkward for him. She secretly hoped it would be.

"The first week in November is fine." Dan rested his chin in his hands and gazed at her thoughtfully. "Just fine."

April wasn't quite sure what to make of that look. He seemed to be assessing her in some way, and her skin prickled in sensual response. Was he engaged or wasn't he? Rude or not, she'd ask him after the meeting. She had a right to know before she skipped blithely up to Chicago and then came face-to-face with the woman.

The meeting ended with Dan asking the others to take various responsibilities for the other projects. April admired the way he handled the delicate matter of directing the three men who were all old enough to be his father, and Bill, who had played football with him and was a friend. April had never noticed Dan's leadership abilities before, and she recognized Irene's influence in the careful way Dan motivated the group to work together. It seemed that Dan's grandmother had known what she was doing when she put him in charge.

At last everyone began pushing back chairs and gathering notes. As the men switched from talk of the endowment to a discussion of the previous night's high-school football game, April edged around the table and touched Dan's arm. "Could I see you for a moment before you head back to Chicago?"

His glance was cheerful. "Sure. I'm not leaving right this minute, anyway. Henry and Mabel have asked me over for lunch."

Figures, April thought. "That's nice," she said aloud. "Then maybe you'd like to drop by the farm on your way out of town? I'll give you a pumpkin to take back to the big city."

He smiled. "We don't have too many trick-or-treaters in my apartment building."

"I didn't mean— Oh, well. It was a stupid idea."

"No. I shouldn't have teased you. I'd love a pumpkin. Maybe I'll even carve it, for old time's sake. Expect me by two, okay?"

She gazed into his eyes. "Okay." Was he remembering that Halloween, so long ago, when he'd come out to the farm with his grandmother to pick out a pumpkin? He'd been fifteen, she thirteen. The two of them had been put in charge of finding the perfect jack-o'-lantern for his grandmother's front porch, and then Irene had suggested they carve it right there, together. The boy and girl, still so young, had laughed and teased each other all the way through the task.

Then the moment had arrived when the laughter stopped, and both she and Dan had sensed the first dim awareness of the man and woman they were becoming, sampled the first taste of wanting. Looking at him now, April knew that she'd never completely lost that yearning for Dan. Perhaps she never would.

APRIL NEEDED all the produce business she could get, but she wished everyone had stayed away that afternoon. Unfortunately for her privacy, the Saturday before Halloween was the perfect time for families to drive into the country in search of the perfect jack-o'-lantern and a sack of apples for dunking in caramel.

Knowing that she'd no doubt have to work that afternoon, April had changed out of her dress and into jeans and a red sweatshirt. She couldn't wear her contacts, either, although the urge was strong to look a little sexier for Dan. But with her glasses on she could see the customers, and with them off she could read the scale when weighing the pumpkins. The contacts were lousy for close work. So much for glamour—as if it mattered. Dan was engaged.

When he arrived a little after two, April's driveway was a busy thoroughfare. She stood in the front yard behind a wooden picnic table that served as a counter for the scale and the cash box. Business was so steady that she scarcely had time to nod hello to Dan as he parked the red Honda and sauntered over.

"Looks like you could use a hand," he said, glancing at the line forming beside the scale. "Let me weigh and you collect the money."

"Don't be silly, Dan." April took a pumpkin the size of a basketball from a little girl and placed it on the scale. "Go on in the kitchen and have some hot cider," she suggested, sliding her glasses down her nose to read the scale. "It's on the stove." She handed the pumpkin back to the little girl and readjusted her glasses before making change from a twenty-dollar bill the girl's father took from his wallet. "The rush should be over in a sec."

"Doesn't look like it. Two more cars just turned in the drive. Besides, if I weigh, you don't have to go through that routine with your glasses, Here." Without asking he took a giant pumpkin from her arms and lowered it to the scale.

"But I didn't ask you out here so that you could work."

He flashed her a smile. "For a city boy this isn't work. Let's see, this one's thirty-two pounds. Now be quiet and take this nice lady's money."

"Good advice," the woman said, handing over the amount April asked for. "And be grateful for the help. Some men of my acquaintance wouldn't even offer, especially if it's a good afternoon for fishing."

April laughed. "True." She thought immediately of her fun-loving Jimmy, who had always seemed to disappear when the time came for chores. Because life on the farm was a constant series of chores, one day he had simply disappeared, period.

She and Dan worked side by side for the next hour without a break. She wondered if he had any reaction at all when they accidentally brushed against each other in the course of waiting on customers. She was acutely aware each time it happened, and her heart raced for several seconds afterward.

*Relax*, she warned herself. *The guy's engaged.* She wondered if she could be the sort of perverse person who didn't want a man until someone else showed an interest. But no, she'd wanted Dan plenty in high school. He just hadn't shared her fervor. If he had, she'd be married to him now.

Married to Dan. April knew the experience would have been totally different from being Jimmy's wife. Partway into their six-year marriage, she'd admitted to herself that Jimmy no longer excited her sexually. It wasn't his fault— unless she counted lack of maturity his fault. She'd tried to change her response. Nothing had worked.

Secretly she believed that had she been a more enthusiastic lover, Jimmy might not have left. Therefore she couldn't blame him for the divorce, although most people in Booneville did. Jimmy's reputation was ruined here; no wonder he'd headed for Oregon.

And today all the passion she hadn't been able to manufacture for poor Jimmy was being whipped into life by the slight friction of Dan's arm against hers, the occasional bump of a thigh. Life wasn't fair.

"April? Sixteen pounds, kiddo."

She blushed and turned away. How many times had Dan repeated himself while the line of customers watched her staring off into space? "Right. Sixteen."

Dan put his head close to hers. "Where were you?"

Thinking about you. About sex. "Daydreaming. I'm sorry."

"Never mind. Don't look now, but we haven't had another car pull up for about five minutes. Maybe the deluge is over for a while." He weighed another pumpkin. "Twenty-one pounds."

"I hope so. The money's nice, but I really wanted to talk with you."

"That's nice. I really wanted to talk with you, too."

She glanced at him. Was he going to discuss his engagement, just to get things straight between them? Maybe he'd noticed something; maybe he knew her well enough to pick up signals she was unwillingly giving off, and he didn't want her to embarrass herself. What a depressing thought.

April waited impatiently for the last customer to pay for his pumpkin while Dan carried two wooden lawn chairs from the front porch and placed them facing each other behind the picnic table.

When they sat down, April felt a moment of panic. Now he would tell her, and she didn't want to know. She waved her hand toward the diminished mound of pumpkins. "I had planned to give you one," she said, staving off his announcement for a little longer. "But the best may be taken."

"Then I'll choose one with character, as my grandmother used to say."

"That's right. She never liked the perfectly round pumpkins, did she?" April smiled at Dan as they shared another memory of the woman they would miss for a long time. When Dan opened his mouth as if to speak again, she hopped to her feet. "Why don't you pick the one you want, while I get us that hot cider I promised you earlier?"

"Bring a knife and a spoon and some newspaper. I've gotten in the mood to carve the face, after all this."

"You're just humoring me."

"No, I'm not. I have to keep in practice, don't I?"

April looked back over her shoulder. "In practice? What for?"

"So I can teach my kids someday."

His statement caught her like a blow to the stomach. She wasn't going to accept the news of this engagement gracefully. "Oh. I suppose so," she mumbled, turning away to walk quickly into the house. He'd probably present his fiancée with the carved pumpkin, and she'd be charmed with this rustic gift, a symbol of the quaint traditions of rural living. Nuts.

When she returned with mugs of cider, and a newspaper tucked under one arm, Dan was drawing a face on a tall skinny pumpkin that sat on the table in front of him.

"I borrowed your pencil from the cash box. What do you think?"

"Looks like M.G. Tucker." April had given herself a talking-to in the kitchen and had vowed to be breezy and unconcerned with Dan. His love life was out of her jurisdiction, and her attraction to him was irrelevant.

"Yeah, especially if I bend some wire to look like glasses. I always thought he was sweet on Grandma. Did you bring the knife?"

April reached into the back pocket of her jeans and pulled out a paring knife and a large spoon. "This should be quite a pumpkin."

"Good therapy." Dan plunged the knife into the orange rind and cut a circle for the top. "I haven't hollowed out a pumpkin since . . ." He glanced at April and then returned to his task. "In years," he finished, twisting off the top and scraping the pearly seeds and stringy pulp onto the newspaper at his feet.

"I've carved one every Halloween." April sat down and picked up her mug of cider. "Except of course when I was out of the country."

For a while the only sound was the scraping of the spoon against the inside of the pumpkin. "Don't you miss it?" Dan said at last while he continued to scrape. "All that traveling?"

"Actually, no."

"Being stuck in one very small town is okay with you?"

"Sure. I finally learned that I'm a small-town girl at heart. I'll take other trips someday, but never for so long at one time. I like Booneville and my life here."

Dan continued to scrape, although the inside of the pumpkin yielded no more seeds or pulp. "You're not lonely?"

April recoiled from the intimate question. What gave him the right to ask it? "Not especially," she lied. Before she'd wanted to postpone talking about his engagement. Now she wished he'd get it over with. "Listen, Dan, I've been thinking about my tour of the galleries in Chicago. Under the circumstances, shouldn't I do that alone? I'll check with you before I make a final selection of sculptors, but you don't have to baby-sit me while I'm investigating the possibilities."

Dan stopped scraping and looked at her. "Under what circumstances? And what makes you think I'd consider it baby-sitting?"

"I'm sure you have more important responsibilities than squiring me around. You have your work, and your set of friends there. I don't want to intrude." *Say it, please. Don't make me drag it out of you.*

His laughter was bemused. "You wouldn't be an intrusion. What is it, April?"

"Dan, I know your mother isn't wearing the ring anymore, so you may as well be frank with me."

"I'd rather be Dan."

"Do you have to make stupid jokes at a time like this? I assume you're getting married, and I . . . don't want to bother you when you're in the midst of wedding plans. Now do you understand?"

"Yes, but you don't."

"What?"

"As a matter of fact, I do have the ring, but I'm not marrying anyone. My mother gave me the ring because . . ."

"Because why?" April's heart beat faster.

He gave her a quizzical smile. "Never mind. Just because. Anyway, I'm perfectly free to 'squire you around,' as you put it. Would you like to stay at the Palmer House? I can get you a discount through my company's corporate account there."

"I . . . I don't know what to say."

"That's a first."

"Dan, stop it. I've had a severe jolt here, thinking you were engaged, and I don't need your smart-aleck remarks."

"Oh?"

April saw an assessing look on his face again and realized how much she'd just given away. She couldn't think of any words with which to call back what she'd said, and she could tell by his searching expression that he wasn't going to leave the subject alone.

He put down the spoon and leaned forward, his blue eyes focusing on her with an intensity that made her tremble with desire. She had never wanted him so much, and she feared that he knew it.

His tone was quiet and controlled. "What *do* you need from me, April?"

# 4

APRIL SWALLOWED. "I don't know what you mean."

"The hell you don't."

"A lot—" Her vocal cords wouldn't work smoothly. She tried again. "A lot has happened between us, Dan."

"And a lot hasn't."

Her pulse thundered in her ears. His meaning was all too clear. "I'm not the same girl you dated in high school."

"I should hope not. I'm hardly the same man, either."

"And . . . and I thought you were getting married."

"You thought wrong."

"Yes." She studied his face, so familiar and yet unknown, too. Eight years of experiences that she hadn't shared were hidden behind those blue eyes. Of course there had been women. Knowing Dan, April imagined the relationships had been serious, passionate . . . and consummated.

How well did he remember those nights after high-school dances when they'd parked along moonlit farm roads and tempted each other, veering away from forbidden pleasure at the last moment? They were adults now. Nothing was forbidden anymore.

Considering the direction of her thoughts, she wasn't surprised when he reached for her, guiding her out of the chair until they were standing, staring silently at each other.

Carefully he took off her glasses and laid them on the
picnic table. Then he framed her face with his hands. "Tell
me what you need."

"Maybe I don't know," she murmured, trembling.

"Maybe we can find out."

As he lowered his head, she closed her eyes. At the soft
caress of his mouth on hers she was catapulted back in time
to those long-ago days of loving Dan, of welcoming the
scent of him, the urgent press of his lips, the whisper of his
breath against her cheek.

At first his touch was agonizingly familiar, and she
could have been fifteen again, sharing their first kiss, declaring the first words of undying love. But his embrace
soon became less tentative, the exploration of his tongue
more demanding. As mature emotions pumped through
her, April realized that innocence was gone forever, for
both of them. Their virginal high-school-sweetheart days
were over, and they knew it.

With some effort at self-control, she pulled away. "Dan,
we're in the middle of my front yard in broad daylight."

"Then let's go inside." He was breathing hard.

April shook her head. "This is too fast."

"Too fast?" He stared at her. Then he began to laugh.
"That's true, I guess. I've only known you for about thirteen years."

"We've been apart, Dan. We have some catching up to
do."

"Could have fooled me. I think we just caught up."

"Dan, I don't want to make any... mistakes."

His expression grew more cautious. "Neither do I, now
that you mention it."

"Maybe my trip to Chicago will give us a chance to get
to know each other again."

He nodded slowly. "Could be."

"Dan, I can't help the way I respond to you. I've always—" She waved her hand in the air, unwilling or unable to explain further. "But other things are important, too, don't you agree?"

"You're asking me? Somehow the lines seem to be reversed from a discussion we had a few years ago. Yes, I agree, dammit. But a few things have changed, as you pointed out. I was pretty good at restraint back in those days. I can't guarantee that kind of control now."

April felt a flash of white-hot desire. Hadn't that been what she had wanted eight years ago, a man driven beyond reason by his passion? Yes, by his passion, but also by his love. That was it. She had no idea how much love figured into all this. And she needed to know.

"I think the Chicago visit will give us a chance to find out a lot of things, Dan."

"I guess you're right. We really haven't spent any time together in the past few years." He regarded her thoughtfully. "What about the hotel? You don't have to stay there, April."

Her body quivered as she imagined heading for Chicago and rushing straight into his arms, into his bed. "Yes, I do."

He nodded. "Then I'll make the reservation. Is a week from Monday what you want?"

She smiled. What she wanted was to be back in his arms right this minute. "That's fine."

He gazed at her without speaking. Then he took a deep breath. "I think I'd be wise to hit the road," he said, picking up his jack-o'-lantern.

"Yes," she said with a fond look. "That's best." She watched him drive away and wondered if she was a damn fool. He would have stayed the weekend if she'd asked. They could be lovers by now. But she'd made one terrible mistake eight years ago. Falling into Dan's arms now would be like a driver who sees danger, overcorrects and smashes into a different obstacle. As much as she hated to admit it, April was learning caution.

THE BEAUTIFY BOONEVILLE committee ordinarily met each Wednesday afternoon in the library, but it hadn't convened since Irene's death. April decided that a meeting was in order, however, before she went to Chicago. She wanted to be sure the committee was behind her.

First she called Ida Mae, who agreed that the women should gather on Wednesday afternoon, as usual. Irene would have expected them to carry on without undue sentimentality, Ida Mae said. She promised to notify Bess Easley if April would get in touch with Mabel Goodpasture.

On Wednesday a storm blew in, stripping the multicolored leaves from the trees and pelting the town with a heavy rain. April parked the truck in front of the library and stepped over the gutter clogged with soggy brown remnants of fall's splendor. She wasn't fond of this cold, wet prelude to winter and often wished the seasons would go directly from the brightness of autumn leaves to the pristine beauty of the snow.

She skirted puddles on the sidewalk as she hurried through the rain to the library's front door. The snow probably wouldn't arrive for another month, she thought, and then the weather might affect her sculpture plans if the artist wanted to do some of the work on the site. Perhaps she'd have to wait until spring to see the culmination of her dream for the square.

Mabel Goodpasture, a well-endowed woman nearing fifty, was already inside shaking the rain from her black umbrella. "Hello, April. I bet I know what we'll be talking about today. Henry said something about money for a statue, and I knew right away you were behind that."

"I think Irene would have wanted us to continue the beautification program for the square, don't you, Mabel?"

"Oh, absolutely. Although Henry isn't very excited about a statue, I can tell you."

"I know."

"But don't let that worry you," Mabel said over her shoulder as she led the way back toward the periodical section of the library where the committee usually met. "We'll bring him around."

"If you say so." April was awed by the change in Mabel since the beautification committee was formed two years ago. Irene's influence could be seen in that, too. Mabel never used to oppose her husband in anything, but Henry's autocratic days were numbered. Rumor had it that they'd already fought over how the house was to be redecorated and where their oldest child would attend college. Would the sculpture be the next topic of dissension?

As April and Mabel approached the reading area, they were greeted by the steady ping of rain falling into several buckets positioned on the floor and both couches.

Myra Gibbons, Booneville's librarian, hurried forward with another pan. "Oh, ladies, the roof in this section has finally given away. You'll have to move to the children's area for your meeting."

Mabel glanced around at the drips. "I'm not surprised. The roof must be at least forty years old."

"It should be replaced," Myra said, positioning her pan under another leak. "I asked M.G. Tucker to put in for that from the Butler money, but I guess we won't get the roof this year. Too many other projects, M.G. said."

April felt her first stab of guilt over the sculpture. Vaguely she remembered M.G. discussing the library's roof, but when the money was nearly all spoken for, he'd suggested that the sculpture receive the last amount. Of course, it hadn't been raining then, and the roof hadn't started to leak.

By the time Ida Mae arrived with tiny, birdlike Bess in tow, April had worked herself into a lather of indecision. She looked at the four of them, sitting in a circle on tiny chairs with their knees almost to their chins. A leaky roof was more important than art, wasn't it?

Ida Mae finished her discussion with Bess about their two oldest boys, who were in the same grade at school. Then she turned toward April. "Ready to start?"

"Why, yes, of course." April realized she'd been waiting because Irene had always opened the discussions. They had no officers, but Irene had been the one who had taken charge of the meetings. Now the three other committee members were looking to her instead.

"Tell Bess about the statue," Mabel prompted. "Bill's already told Ida Mae, I'm sure."

"Well . . ." April twisted her hands together. "As you remember, Irene and I had talked about a sculpture for the square, something for the northeast corner that would balance the gazebo on the southwest corner. We didn't have any money for it, but on Saturday the board that is handling Irene's estate income voted an amount for that purpose."

"Terrific!" Bess clapped her hands.

"But now I wonder if we should take it," April added. "You all saw the buckets when you came in. The new library roof wasn't approved for this year, but the sculpture was."

# What is sexy?

*Jōvan® Musk.*

JOVAN
MUSK
FOR MEN

AFTERSHAVE / COLOGNE

4 FL OZ / 118.4 ML

JOVAN
MUSK

*What sexy is.*

# SAVE UP TO $2.00
# FOR YOU <u>AND</u> THE MAN YOU LOVE
# ON JŌVAN MUSK!

## SAVE $1.00

### JŌVAN. MUSK
### FOR MEN

**TO THE RETAILER:** For each coupon you accept from the customer at time of purchase of any Jōvan Musk for Men item, Jōvan will pay you $1.00 plus 8¢ handling if terms of offer have been complied with by you and the consumer. Presentation for redemption without such compliance constitutes fraud. Payment will be made only to retailers stocking these products. Invoices proving purchase of sufficient stock to cover coupons presented for redemption must be shown upon request. Coupons may not be assigned or transferred. Any sales tax must be paid by the consumer. Offer good only in the U.S.A. and void where prohibited, licensed, taxed or restricted by law. Cash value 1/20 of 1¢. Unauthorized reproduction of this coupon is prohibited. For payment, mail coupon to Jōvan, Inc., P.O. Box 14851, Chicago, Illinois 60614. **Offer expires 3/31/89. Consumer Note:** Limit one coupon per purchase of any Jōvan Musk for Men item. **Consumer must complete information below to redeem coupon.** This information will be kept confidential.

NAME _____

ADDRESS _____

CITY _____ STATE _____ ZIP _____

H

5  35017 12276  1

**MANUFACTURER'S COUPON – EXPIRES 3/31/89**

---

## SAVE $1.00

### JŌVAN. MUSK
### FOR WOMEN

**TO THE RETAILER:** For each coupon you accept from the customer at time of purchase of any Jōvan Musk for Women item, Jōvan will pay you $1.00 plus 8¢ handling if terms of offer have been complied with by you and the consumer. Presentation for redemption without such compliance constitutes fraud. Payment will be made only to retailers stocking these products. Invoices proving purchase of sufficient stock to cover coupons presented for redemption must be shown upon request. Coupons may not be assigned or transferred. Any sales tax must be paid by the consumer. Offer good only in the U.S.A. and void where prohibited, licensed, taxed or restricted by law. Cash value 1/20 of 1¢. Unauthorized reproduction of this coupon is prohibited. For payment, mail coupon to Jōvan, Inc., P.O. Box 14851, Chicago, Illinois 60614. **Offer expires 3/31/89. Consumer Note:** Limit one coupon per purchase of any Jōvan Musk for Women item. **Consumer must complete information below to redeem coupon.** This information will be kept confidential.

NAME _____

ADDRESS _____

CITY _____ STATE _____ ZIP _____

H

5  35017 12376  8

**MANUFACTURER'S COUPON – EXPIRES 3/31/89**

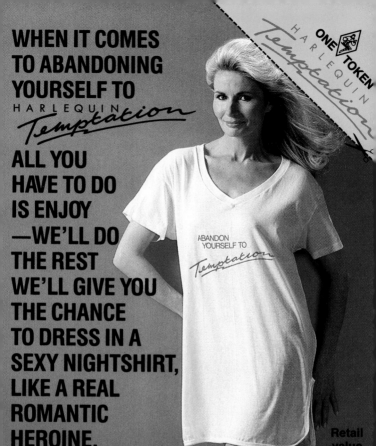

# WHEN IT COMES TO ABANDONING YOURSELF TO

HARLEQUIN *Temptation*

# ALL YOU HAVE TO DO IS ENJOY —WE'LL DO THE REST WE'LL GIVE YOU THE CHANCE TO DRESS IN A SEXY NIGHTSHIRT, LIKE A REAL ROMANTIC HEROINE.

*We'll provide a fascinating, handsome hero or four.* You'll find them on our incredibly sensual new covers, starting this month.

*We'll make it all so easy.* All you have to do is read and dream of that special moment when you abandon yourself to Temptation. Collect your 2, 3 or 5 Harlequin Temptation tokens, fill in the coupon below, and send the tokens and the coupon with your check or money order to Harlequin—your nightshirt will arrive before the last kiss is even faded from your memory! Offer ends December 31, 1988.

*And we'll show you a way to share the moment with the one you love.* The finishing touch is on the next page: an offer on deliciously provocative fragrance that adds to the fantasy— for you and your man....

---

✂

Mabel sat up straighter in her tiny chair. "Oh, we have to have the statue. Let one of Henry's projects wait if we need a new library roof."

April almost laughed but knew she didn't dare. Mabel was absolutely serious about her rebellion. If Henry said the sky was blue, she'd claim it was purple with a completely straight face.

"I have a thought," Ida Mae said. "Bill told me which projects were approved, and I bet if each one of the amounts, including the money for the sculpture, were shaved by, say, ten percent, the library roof could be replaced, too."

"Sure, that sounds good," Bess said immediately. "What do you think, April?"

"I think it will be difficult to find a good sculptor with the money we have now, let alone a smaller amount."

"In all of Chicago?" Ida Mae protested. "Come on, now. I know you and Dan will find someone, even for less money."

Bess looked confused. "What's this about April and Dan in Chicago?"

What indeed? April thought, but she quickly composed her features and explained the plan for selecting a sculptor to Bess, the only one without a connection to the board. "I wanted this meeting," April added, "to make sure the committee trusts me to choose someone."

"Of course we trust you," Bess said. "You've been all over Europe, which is more than the rest of us can say."

"But I'm going next year," Mabel said, squaring her shoulders. "I've tagged along on my last Michigan hunting vacation. Henry can come with me to Europe, or he can go to Michigan alone and shoot things."

Bess stared at Mabel. "You'd go to Europe all by yourself?"

"If I have to."

"My goodness." Bess looked as if she couldn't imagine such independence. Bess was sweet, but not terribly bright, in April's opinion. Irene's brand of spunk hadn't transferred itself to Bess.

"I still wonder if we shouldn't give the whole amount to the library," April said, leaning her chin on her hands. "What do you think Irene would have wanted?"

"Everything," Ida Mae said. "The whole ball of wax."

"Probably," April agreed. "Okay, I'll propose this ten-percent cut to the other members of the board. Somebody will have to call Dan."

"You can do that," Ida Mae said with a wave of her hand.

April lifted an eyebrow in Ida Mae's direction. Her friend was pretty quick to suggest that April be the go-between. "Is there any more business we have to discuss?" she said, changing the subject.

"I think we're out of commission until spring, don't you, April?" asked Mabel. "Except for mulching the flower beds before the first snow and hiring some kids to rake leaves, the statue is about all we can do during the winter. Next spring we can start a campaign for all the businesses on the square to spruce up. I've already told Henry that the bank needs new awnings, and in some other color besides that putrid green."

"Shall we still meet every week?" April glanced around the group.

"Absolutely," Mabel said. "Even if we can't physically do things, we can plan for warmer weather. Besides, I like getting together."

"So do I," added Bess. "I enjoy the feeling of doing something for Booneville. Let's keep meeting."

"That's fine with me," April said. "Of course next week I'll be in Chicago, but the week after that I'll be anxious to tell you about the trip."

"And we'll want to hear everything," said Bess with a smile. "I think it sounds exciting."

A sudden churning sensation in April's stomach reminded her that Chicago would indeed be exciting. She also doubted that she'd be telling the Beautify Booneville committee everything about her trip.

THE COOL AUTUMN WEATHER seemed to sharpen the edges of the landscape as April merged her old pickup truck with the hundreds of other vehicles funneling into Chicago on Interstate Fifty-seven. After driving the farm roads around Booneville for the past two years, April felt inadequate to the task of navigating the multilaned expressway choked with vehicles, but she was determined to take the Outer Drive and see the water. Lake Michigan was the best thing about Chicago, as far as April was concerned.

She didn't dare take more than occasional glances at the white-capped blue water on her right as she was propelled along with the traffic, but she knew it was there, just the same. The freshness of the lake and the breeze that blew almost continuously from it seemed to sweep Chicago clean of the grime that hung over many other big cities she'd visited.

On her left towered the gray giants of the Chicago skyline, the man-made peaks from which financial wizards viewed their kingdom. April always got vertigo when she walked down Michigan Avenue and looked up to the top of the tall buildings. Through an optical illusion they appeared to lean precariously over the street as if ready to crash down on her at any moment.

She realized that the same illusion made straight rows of corn seem to fan out on the near side of the field and gather to a point on the other. It was called perspective. April preferred the perspective of the fields. Only the expanse of Lake Michigan provided her with the serenity she felt when gazing across acres of farmland punctuated only by telephone poles, occasional windbreaks of trees and an isolated grain elevator.

April watched for the first left turn that would take her over to Wabash Avenue and the Palmer House. She'd timed her arrival so that she could check right in, and then she was supposed to call Dan. Her hands trembled as she shifted the truck into a lower gear to take the turn. Somewhere in Chicago was Dan Butler, at home here, not awed by the big city as April still was, even after all her travels abroad. Dan's presence nearby was both reassuring and unsettling. How would her life be changed when she drove away from the city five days from now? Certainly it would not be the same.

The valet at the entrance accepted the keys to her battered truck without a trace of a smile, and a bellhop appeared immediately to take her suitcase, scarred from her vagabond existence with Jimmy. For a brief moment April longed for Booneville's unpretentious way of life, where what she wore and how much she tipped had no relevance.

As she stepped into the lobby, she was glad for the quick shopping trip to Springfield that had yielded the calf-length wool skirt she wore with a very fashionable pair of boots and a soft angora sweater. A few other clothing purchases nestled in the old suitcase that the bellhop carried toward the check-in counter for her. April was determined not to be a hick, not in front of the sculptors she would interview and certainly not in front of Dan. She had forsaken her glasses in favor of her contact lenses for the occasion.

The room was five floors up and had a view of the street below, an amenity not lost on April. Some of the hotel's windows, she knew, looked out on the buildings at either side. Dan had wanted her to have something nicer than that. She realized that she'd missed his brand of thoughtfulness, had almost forgotten what it was like to be cared for in this way.

The room exuded understated elegance through muted colors and dark woods glowing from years of careful polishing. The heavy drapes and thickly carpeted floors hushed the sound within and without so that April could close her eyes and almost forget she was in the middle of a city.

Except she couldn't because the room had the scent of the city, not the farm. Even up here, five stories above the street, she caught the acrid smell of car exhaust. Gone was the fragrance of wet earth turned by a plow, of mown hay in late summer and wood fires in the winter. She couldn't live here, not ever. How did Dan manage?

"Will that be all?" the bellhop asked, placing her suitcase gingerly on the floor as if he feared it might come apart.

"Yes, thank you." April was proud of the way she handed him the tip she had ready in her hand, although she hated the whole process of shoving money at people. Mentally she recorded another strike against city living, where tipping was a way of life. But she was here for five days only, and she could play the game for that long.

When the bellhop left, she rummaged through her purse for Dan's number at work and picked up the receiver of the bedside telephone. This was the third time in a week she'd talked to him on the phone. Last Wednesday night she'd called about shaving ten percent of the funding from the other town projects. After some communication back and forth among the other board members, Dan called her to say everyone was in agreement.

Their conversations had been lean, indicating that neither was willing to wander from the subject of business into the murky waters of their personal lives. There was so much to say, and the telephone didn't seem the way to say it.

A receptionist came on the line at Adonis Sporting Goods and switched April to Dan's office. April tried to picture him there, sitting behind a desk, working with sales reports. Her Dan. *Her Dan?* Where had that come from?

"Dan Butler speaking. May I help you?"

"It's me, Dan. I'm here."

His tone changed from efficient courtesy to genuine warmth. "I thought it might be you. I've been watching the clock. How was the drive?"

After their straightforward conversations last week she hadn't expected this intimate kind of greeting. "Fine," she stammered. "No, not fine, crazy. I should have driven a tractor up here so that I could intimidate some of those kamikaze nuts on the Outer Drive."

Dan laughed. "Is the truck parked now?"

"And for the next five days, thank you. I placed the keys in the gloved hand of the valet. I doubt he's ever driven such a vintage model into the parking garage of the Palmer House."

"Probably not."

"Anyway, it's shoe leather and taxis for me."

"Or my Honda. In fact, I'd hoped to chauffeur you to some galleries this afternoon, but the boss called a sales meeting."

"That's okay. I'll walk to the ones close to the hotel. No problem." She hoped her disappointment wasn't evident in her voice. Of course he had a job, and she shouldn't have expected that he'd pop over here the minute she picked up the phone.

"Dinner, then? Let me take you out somewhere."

"That would be nice but certainly not necessary if you—"

"I thought we were going to get to know each other while you're here?"

"Uh, yes, I suppose we did say that."

"Changed your mind?"

"No. I'd . . . I'd love to have dinner."

"I'll be there at seven."

"Great." She hung up the phone and immediately ran for her suitcase. This was definitely the night for the black slinky thing she'd found at the last minute during her Springfield shopping spree. She'd shown her mother everything she'd picked out except that dress. One look at that black number and her mother would have wondered what April had in mind for this Chicago trip. Until April had decided about Dan, she didn't want her mother getting funny ideas.

She checked the black dress for wrinkles before hanging it and everything else on the attached wooden hangers in the closet. No wire for this place. Then she checked her watch and discovered she still had several hours to kill before seven o'clock. She might as well spend them doing what she'd told Dan she'd be doing—touring the nearby art galleries. She grabbed her purse and room key and left.

THREE HOURS LATER, as she limped along in the deep shadows of Michigan Avenue in the late afternoon, she cursed herself for hiking around in her new boots before they'd been broken in. By the time she'd realized her problem, it was too late. She debated taking a cab for the last six blocks and decided that was a foolish waste of money.

Back in her room, as she eased the boots from her battered feet and peeled off her nylons, she wished she'd taken the cab. Maybe then the blisters wouldn't have broken.

The bathwater stung her feet, but she hoped somehow to salvage the situation enough to put on the black high heels that went with her dress. Fresh from her bath and feeling a little better, she dressed in black panties and bra and applied her makeup. Then, as a last test before putting on her dress, she gathered the left leg of a pair of black patterned panty hose and tried to ease the material over her foot.

April wasn't a real fan of physical pain. With a yelp she removed the intrument of torture from her foot. If she couldn't stand the stockings, what hope was there for three-inch sling pumps? None, that's what. She couldn't go to dinner tonight, unless Dan favored places that allowed the patrons to dine in bare feet. And she had been so determined not be a hayseed here in the big city. She was willing to bet that a Chicago woman wouldn't march twenty-five blocks in a new pair of boots.

She tried to call Dan at his apartment, but he'd apparently already left. She could do nothing but tell him when he arrived that she'd take a rain check on his offer. Should she admit the truth or invent some excuse about a headache? She was debating the issue when the telephone rang.

"April?"

"Hi, Dan. I was trying to call you."

"I'm in the lobby. Should I come up, or would you rather meet me down here?"

She'd intended to put him off with the headache excuse, but the sound of his voice filled her with yearning. Dammit, she wanted to be with him, blisters or no blisters. "Well, to tell you the truth . . ." She stalled, searching for a way out of her dilemma. Then her gaze fell upon the leather-bound menu on the walnut writing desk.

"To tell you the truth, Dan," she said, making her decision, "I think it might be more fun to order room service tonight, don't you?"

# 5

DAN HESITATED only a fraction of a second. "Sure, why not? I can cancel our reservations from your room."

That fraction of a second proved long enough for April to understand what her suggestion must mean to him. She'd invited him to spend the evening in the privacy of her room. Her room had a bed in it.

Well, was making love to him what she wanted tonight? And if so, what about all that talk about "getting to know each other" before taking this precipitous step?

April admitted to herself that she had no idea what she was doing. Maybe the room-service idea had sprung from a natural urge to conceal her stupidity about her new boots. Then again, maybe her subconscious desire to make love to Dan had thrown the suggestion forward, masked as a clever ploy to save her pride.

What now? Dan was on his way up, and she was dressed in her underwear. If she didn't put on some clothes, her decision about the tone of the evening would be made pretty quickly by the man ascending in the hotel elevator.

Until she knew her own mind better, she'd forget the slinky black dress. That would have been fine in a crowded restaurant, but not under the present circumstances. She debated quickly, expecting his knock on the door at any minute.

After rummaging through her limited choices, she finally grabbed a pair of brown wool slacks and a tailored apricot-colored blouse of a material that imitated silk. She pulled the clothes quickly over her black underwear. The elevators must be busy, she thought, when Dan hadn't yet arrived. She took the extra time to brush her hair and check her makeup.

For her tortured feet she chose her comfortable fluffy slippers. Then, when Dan still wasn't at the door, she added the last touch. Racing into the bathroom, she took out her contacts and replaced them with her glasses. There. She looked casual yet conservative, sweet instead of sexy.

The knock came at last, and she gulped with nervousness. What did one say to reverse the thoughts of a man who thought he'd been subtly propositioned? April elected to say nothing and let her appearance speak for her.

From his shocked expression when she opened the door, April figured that her appearance must have spoken volumes. She almost laughed as he stared in disbelief at her slacks, blouse and fluffy slippers. She wondered if his fantasy had been a revealing negligee, sexy loungewear, or perhaps Saran Wrap and a smile.

He, on the other hand, had worn the perfect counterpart to her black dress. A topcoat was folded over one arm, and April noticed that he looked even better in a tux now than the first and only time she'd seen him wear one—at the senior prom when they broke up.

"I stopped at the bar and ordered a bottle of wine to be sent up," he began uncertainly. "Should I cancel the order?"

"Why?"

"Well, I—" He stopped speaking, apparently unable to admit that the wine had been part of a seduction scene that he now doubted would take place.

His discomfort bothered her. He was, after all, an old friend and deserved to know exactly why she'd suggested this intimate dinner. "Oh, Dan, come in and sit down. I'll explain everything. Let me take your coat. In fact, both your coats. I've caused you to dress up for no reason, all because of my own stupidity."

"What stupidity?" He handed her his tux jacket and his topcoat.

"I'll tell you when we're settled." She wondered what it was about a white pleated shirt and a black satin cummerbund that were so compelling. Maybe she hadn't seen enough men dressed up like this, and the novelty of formal clothes attracted her. To avoid acting like a hayseed, she'd better not stand around staring, either. She walked to the closet and hung both coats on hangers.

"Shall I ditch the tie, too?"

April turned around. "That's the kind you have to tie yourself, isn't it?" she asked with a grimace. "I'll bet you spent ten minutes getting it right."

"Twelve."

"I feel like a jerk."

"Don't." Dan pulled the tie until the two ends dangled on either side of the row of pearly studs down the middle of the shirt. Then he unfastened the collar button and took out the first stud and put it in his pocket. "But I'd sure like to know what's going on. What's the matter?"

Nothing, April thought, watching him take the studs from his cuffs and roll the shirtsleeves back over his muscular forearms. Talk about making lemonade from lemons. If Dan looked handsome in the tux, he looked sexy as hell half out of it. She wasn't sure what she was doing, but she liked the way it was turning out.

"Well, I did something dumb," April began, crossing to the small table and two chairs positioned by the window. "I'll show you." She sat down and eased off one of her slippers. "Look at this."

Dan crossed to the chair and glanced down at her foot. "Ouch." He knelt in front of her and took the blistered foot in both hands. "You'll never make it to the ball this way, Cinderella."

She repressed a shiver of delight as he cradled her foot in his palm and examined the broken skin on her heel and her little toe. "I knew I should have turned one of those pumpkins into a coach before I left the farm."

He glanced up from his appraisal. "New shoes?"

April nodded. "Boots. You'd think I was a kid on the first day of school. Remember how we used to suffer after a barefoot summer? The first day we'd wear our new shoes and then limp around slathered in Band-Aids for days afterward."

He rubbed his thumb tenderly along her instep. "I hope you had some luck at the art galleries, considering how you sacrificed your feet this afternoon."

"Not really." She tried to keep her tone light, although it wasn't easy while he was stroking her foot like that. "I've learned that finding a sculptor willing to work for the amount we have to spend won't be easy."

"You didn't come up with any names at all?"

"Not this time out."

"Poor April." Without warning, he bent and placed his lips against the vein that ran across the top of her foot.

"Dan!" The touch of his mouth on such an unexpected part of her body brought a rush of desire that embarrassed her. "Don't be silly," she protested with faint conviction, pulling her foot away.

He placed both hands on his knees and gazed at her steadily, his blue eyes smoldering. "Are you afraid of me, April?"

"Why would you think such a ridiculous thing?" She smoothed the fur of the slipper with her hands to stop them from trembling. "I've known you practically forever."

"That's not what you said when I saw you last, after the big pumpkin sale. You said a lot of time had gone by, and we didn't know each other well at all. You acted afraid then, too."

"That wasn't afraid, that was cautious."

He lifted a dark eyebrow. "Cautious? You?"

"Yes, sometimes. I told you I'm not the same person I was eight years ago."

"Is that why you're dressed like a schoolteacher tonight?"

April straightened in the chair. "I'm sorry if you're disappointed. I have a limited supply of clothes, and this happens to be—"

"The least provocative thing you could find on short notice. I'm glad you didn't have more time before I arrived. You might have spread cream on your face and put your hair up in rollers."

"You're exaggerating."

"And the glasses, April. The glasses are a dead giveaway. We may have been apart for eight years, but there are some things I remember very well. One is that you hide behind those glasses when you don't want anybody to think of you as a sexy woman. It may work for the general public, but as for—"

A knock at the door interrupted him.

"The wine. What timing." Dan sighed and got to his feet. "Maybe it's good timing, at that. The situation seems to call for it."

"What situation?"

Dan half turned on his way to the door. "Getting to know you, Mrs. Foster."

*Mrs. Foster.* In point of fact that's who she was, although hearing it from Dan, spoken in that tone, made her cringe. She wished now that she'd asked the judge to reinstate her maiden name, but she hadn't thought of it at the time of her divorce.

While Dan answered the door, April looked down at her feet, one bare and one clad in a fluffy slipper. She took the other slipper off. Why was everything so complicated all of a sudden, just because she'd got blisters on her feet and couldn't go out? But things *were* complicated, and signals were getting mixed, partly because she had no clear idea of where she wanted to go from here.

The waiter entered the room bearing the wine and two glasses on a tray balanced head-high. He placed the tray with a flourish on the table next to April. She felt slightly uncomfortable with this stranger in the room. Was he wondering what the arrangement was here, with the room in her name and a man keeping her company in it? Probably not. He was paid not to wonder anything. This was the big city, not Booneville, she reminded herself. People's private lives belonged to them alone.

Still, she stood and padded over to the desk containing the room-service menu. "We may as well order now, don't you think?" she asked Dan in a tone meant to convey casual friendship instead of rampant passion.

"If you like," he replied, watching her carefully.

April looked at the waiter. "Can you take our order for dinner?"

"Certainly, ma'am."

"Then I'll have this." She pointed absently to an item under the entrées before handing the menu to Dan.

"I'll have the same," he said, closing the leather cover and tossing the menu back on the desk.

"Very good, sir." The waiter handed Dan a glass with a small amount of wine in the bottom.

"You'd better let her taste it." Dan motioned to April. "She's been to Europe, and she knows more about this than I do."

April glanced at him. One thing was becoming clear to her. They'd have to discuss her marriage to Jimmy. She waved the glass away. "I'm sure it's fine."

"Very well." The waiter poured their glasses half-full and set the bottle on the tray. As he headed for the door, Dan followed him, murmuring a few things April couldn't hear while he handed over the tip.

After closing the door, Dan returned to the table and picked up his glass. "To Auld Lang Syne."

April touched her glass to his. "To new discoveries."

"You can't make discoveries if you're afraid," he reminded her gently.

"Cautious."

"Right. Cautious." He sipped his wine.

"I'd...I'd like to tell you about him, Dan. About Jimmy."

He looked away. "I'm not sure I want to hear."

"Yes, you do. Some of this must be said, or it will fester between us forever. Can't we sit here at this table and bring each other up-to-date like normal friends who've been separated?"

"Is that what we were, normal friends? Funny, but I thought we were more than that to each other, once upon a time, before the clock struck midnight and the coachman turned into a rat."

April saw the hurt still lingering behind his offhand response. After eight years her defection still had the power to bring pain to his eyes. Well, if that weren't so, would they have any basis for building something again? Hurt and anger were better than indifference, weren't they?

She put her hand on his arm and felt the tenseness there. "We were more than just friends," she said softly. "That's why we have to talk about it, about what happened, if we're ever to be more than friends again."

"Okay." Dan sighed and sat down, curling his spine against the rigid lines of the chair. "Tell me about Jimmy Foster. Tell me why I shouldn't hate his guts."

"If you're going to hate anyone, you should hate me," April said, pacing in front of him. "I encouraged Jimmy."

His question, the one that must have burned in him for eight years, came roaring forth like thunder. "Why, dammit?"

"Because I thought you didn't want me."

"Good God."

"Or didn't want me enough," she amended. "Enough to ask me to marry you right then so that we could be together. Oh, Dan, I'd had enough of waiting, of wanting and not having."

"And you thought I hadn't? You thought you were the only one fighting your hormones in the backseat of that old Chevy? When I think of all the times that I almost—"

"But you didn't because you always maintained your control. I both admired and hated that quality in you."

"Me, too. Especially after all that waiting and Jimmy Foster stepped in."

There it was, spelled out. She supposed Dan had a right to be bitter, when after all his nights of stern resolve, Jimmy Foster became her first lover. She poured herself another glass of wine while she debated whether to tell him the most important part of all. "Would it matter to know that my . . . relationship . . . with him wasn't very satisfying?"

His glare was chilling. "No." Silence. "Yes, dammit, I suppose so. If I were a nobler sort, I'd be sorry that you had a rotten time with him, but I'm not that noble. I'm glad that Jimmy Foster wasn't all that you'd hoped when you rode off with him on that ridiculous tractor covered with crepe paper."

"You heard about that?"

"You hear about everything in Booneville. Except what you just told me about your private life with him. I have to assume I'm the first person you've ever told, or I'd probably have heard that, too."

"You are the first person. I'm a little ashamed—no, a lot ashamed—that I wasn't a better wife to Jimmy. He had reason to leave, Dan."

He shook his head. "I can't imagine how he could leave, once he had you. I couldn't imagine anyone being that kind of fool."

"That's because you don't know how I was. After the first year or so, when the infatuation had worn off, I dreaded having him touch me. My parents wondered why we didn't have any kids. They didn't know that we seldom had sex, and when we did, I insisted on birth control. I didn't want his children. I kept telling myself that things would get better, but they didn't. He finally left."

Dan closed his eyes, masking his own pain and the sympathy he didn't want to feel for another man. "Poor bastard," he said at last.

"Yes." April sank to the chair opposite him. "There isn't much more to tell about me. The strange thing is, I think your story may be happier than mine, although you took the greater blow eight years ago."

"Maybe you're right." Dan stared into his wineglass, not speaking for several minutes. "I didn't have your problem, anyway. I went beyond the infatuation point at least twice, but..." He swallowed the last of his wine and gazed at her.

"What?"

"Never mind." He set his glass on the table. "So marrying Jimmy was only a maneuver to get back at me because I didn't want you enough, or so you thought. If I had swept you off your feet, if I had lost control just once in the backseat of that Chevy..."

"The story would have been different," April said softly.

"Are you telling me that my care and consideration for our future landed us in this mess?"

"At eighteen I wanted impetuosity, Dan." April smiled ruefully and looked away. "Perhaps I still do, a little, even at twenty-seven."

Dan rose from his chair. "All right, dammit, I can be just as—" Another knock sounded at the door and Dan paused. "Our dinner just arrived."

"Yes, I think so."

"I guess we should let the man in."

"I guess we should." April gazed at his retreating back with a stab of disappointment. Had she expected that he'd send the waiter back to the kitchen and throw her on the bed after her declared need for spontaneity? Maybe. But he hadn't exactly done that, although for a minute she thought he might have been close.

The waiter carefully created a romantic setting by turning down lamps and lighting candles on the table he wheeled into the room. After he left, April glanced at Dan in appreciation. "This is really lovely. I've never had a candlelit dinner in my own hotel room before. You arranged this with him, didn't you?"

"Yes, but I have the strangest feeling that you might have wanted me to do something else a minute ago."

"Nonsense. This is wonderful."

Dan held her chair. "I guess it's a little more impressive than Jesse's Café."

"Just a little."

For a moment, as Dan hesitated with his hands still resting on the back of her chair, April wondered if he was still thinking about whether to forget dinner. Then he removed his hands and walked to his side of the linen-covered table.

Her sigh of disappointment was so faint that he couldn't have heard, yet he gave her a piercing glance as he sat down and unfolded his napkin. She followed suit, smoothing the soft cloth into her lap before picking up her fork. Then she began to laugh.

"What's funny?"

"I just realized that I ordered chicken."

"You didn't know what we were getting?"

"I wasn't paying much attention. I sort of closed my eyes and chose something. Apparently I chose chicken, of all things, although this is the most exotic-looking chicken dish I've ever seen."

"At these prices, I should hope so."

"Don't worry. I'm paying for this as part of my room bill."

He looked at her. "Who said you were paying for the room?"

"Now wait a minute, Dan."

"No, *you* wait a minute. These five days are on me."

"I'm not sure I like that. I'd feel too much like a kept woman if I accepted such generosity."

"How you feel is entirely up to you."

"Is it?"

"That's right. This is your room, not mine. I, uh, think maybe I owe you a few days at the Palmer House."

"Owe me? What on earth do you mean?"

"Don't you remember?" he asked softly.

She frowned, searching for the meaning of his tender look. Then she found it. "Oh, Lord. Of course." So many years ago, when they were both still in high school, two young lovers had planned the distant prospect of their honeymoon and picked the most elegant place they had ever heard of—the Palmer House in Chicago. In the turbulent times that followed, April had forgotten about the honeymoon, especially when Dan hadn't proposed on the night of the prom.

She gazed at the mature man sitting across from her. In another year he'd be thirty. Already faint lines crinkled at the corners of his eyes, and his smile lines were deepening, too. "We were so young, Dan."

"I guess we were." He laid down his fork and folded his napkin. "And I loved you more than anything in life."

His statement hit her like a blow. He had loved her more than anything in life, and she had thrown that love back in his face when she married another. Her appetite for the gourmet dinner was gone, and obviously so was his. Her words came out almost as a whisper. "I . . . I don't suppose there's any forgiving what I did, is there?"

"Yes, there is." He pushed back his chair and stood up. "But I think we've raked each other over the coals enough for one night."

She wasn't sure what to expect until he turned from her and walked toward the closet. Then she realized he was leaving. Leaving? She sat there, churning with indecision. Hadn't she wanted some time for just what had happened tonight, for some communication, some understanding between them before they made a decision whether to become closer than friends?

"I'll call you tomorrow. Maybe I'll be able to get the afternoon off, and we can tour some galleries together. And take a taxi if you go out, will you? Those feet are a mess."

With that he was gone. She stared at the closed door, stunned that he would disappear so quickly, so irrevocably. The candles still flickered on the table. More than half their meal remained on their plates, uneaten. Gradually she became aware of an aching sense of loss and realized that she had made a decision about how this evening would end, and it wasn't like this.

Throwing her napkin down, she bolted from the table and raced across the plush carpet to the door. Flinging it open, she dashed down the hall to the elevator and punched the button. Could she possibly catch him?

The elevator next to her slid open, but the arrows indicated it was going up, not down. She turned back impatiently to the one in front of her. "Come on, dammit," she muttered.

"Going somewhere?"

She spun at the sound of his voice. "Dan!"

"You crazy, barefoot woman."

She hurtled across the space between them, and he crushed her in his arms.

## 6

THEY CLUNG TO EACH OTHER, laughing between kisses, working around the impediment of her glasses until Dan took them off with a growl of frustration.

"You might as well not use these with me, April," he said, tucking them in the pocket of his topcoat before gathering her close once more. "They don't work."

"What? I can see perfectly well with—"

"You know what I mean," he said, nuzzling behind her ear.

"Yes." His caresses made her breathless. "I never wanted them to work, anyway. But I didn't know that until you left."

"As you notice, I haven't left. I couldn't." Dan gazed into her flushed face. "I should. I should go this minute. Oh, April—"

"Come back to the room." She caught his hand and tugged. "Your dinner's getting cold."

"To hell with my dinner." He slipped his arm around her waist and held her against his side as they walked down the hall.

"That's what I wanted you to say the first time."

"I know it. Don't you think I know it?" He tilted his head back in frustration. "Butler, will you ever learn?"

"You came back, Dan. That counts for something."

"I hope so. I need all the points I can get."

They stepped through the door that April had left open when she ran to the elevator. She glanced at him sheepishly. "I didn't even close and lock the door. Pretty irresponsible, huh?"

Dan nudged the door shut with his foot and tipped her face up to his. "Do you honestly expect me to complain because you wanted me so much that you raced out of here without locking up?"

"I did want you so much," she admitted, losing all false pride as she witnessed the unchecked desire blazing in his eyes.

He touched her cheek with his open palm, and she realized he was trembling. "You need to know something because I don't always have the sense to tell you. I want you just as much, April. Every bit as much." He took a deep, steadying breath. "And now let's lock that door." He released her long enough to hang the Do Not Disturb sign on the front knob. Then he closed and locked the door.

Taking off his coat and tux jacket, he dropped them across the desk chair. Then he eliminated the distance between them and drew her close. "Let's start over."

She gazed up at him, questioning.

"Just for tonight," he said with a smile. "I'm not asking either of us to go back eight years. I doubt if we could."

"Probably not. But sometimes . . ."

"Yeah, me, too." He traced the line of her eyebrow. "God, but you're beautiful."

"I don't . . . think you've ever told me that."

"I haven't?"

April shook her head.

His lips hovered above hers, and his breath was warm and sweet on her face. "Then forgive me for being an idiot. A very young idiot."

"Perhaps we both can forgive, Dan."

He lowered his head. "I can't think of a better way to start than this."

She met the open hunger of his lips with her own. Greedily they tasted each other, tongues exploring in patterns established long ago, patterns now vested with new urgency and meaning. This time, at last, there would be no stopping.

April splayed her fingers across the pleated front of Dan's white shirt and stroked the muscled breadth of his chest. He groaned in response, reaching for the hem of her blouse to tug it from the waistband of her slacks. As he slipped both hands beneath the fabric and gripped her waist to mold her against his body, April gasped at the wild surging of a desire that she'd almost forgotten could exist.

Fitting her pelvis to his, she brushed against his aroused manhood. Long ago this pulsing hardness beneath the material of his trousers had frightened her a little, but now she ached for the completion promised by his fullness pressing against her.

"All those nights in the Chevy," Dan murmured, working down the buttons of her blouse. "Do you remember? I lived for those few moments when I could touch your breasts and love you that much, at least. Even though I knew the agony I'd face, trying to hold back from doing more, I was crazy for those magic times."

"So was I. You made me a little crazy, too. Your hands felt so good."

"You remember?" He pushed her blouse off her shoulders and away from her and unfastened the front clasp of her bra.

"I've never forgotten. Oh, Dan . . ." She moaned as he cupped one of her breasts in his palm and stroked the tip with his thumb.

He kissed her lips and tasted the salt of her tears. "Don't cry," he murmured.

"I've . . . I've missed you."

"I hope so."

"All those wasted years . . ."

"Don't think of that now. Don't think at all." He unfastened her slacks, and they slid to the floor. She stepped out of them and kicked them away. Then with a quick shrug she discarded her bra.

He stood back, needing to see her, for the first time, in the light. He sucked in his breath. Women like April were the reason artists painted nudes, he thought. The round perfection of her breasts was something he'd only guessed at in the dim interior of the Chevy. She was a study in symmetry, with her narrow waist and gently flared hips.

He gazed at the triangle of black lace that mapped the last uncharted territory, the place he'd never dared to go during those nights when they'd steamed up the car windows with their youthful passion. Black lace. What had she been imagining when she chose to wear it tonight? His voice was hoarse. "You're . . . magnificent."

His words seemed to startle her into shyness. "I'm not eighteen anymore. I'm afraid that I'm not as—"

"Yes, you are," he said unsteadily, fighting the urge to rip the last barrier away. Instead, he gathered her close until her breasts pushed against the crisp white of his shirt. "You're more. You're not a fragile young girl now."

"I was never fragile," she murmured, kissing the cleft in his chin. "You just thought so. Sometimes you treated me like a china doll."

With a groan he kissed her hard, plunging his tongue into her mouth, as if to tell her that time was over. His hand swept downward, pulling the lower half of her body tight against the ache that was becoming unbearable. The texture of the material stretching across her silken skin was an affront to his touch, but he knew it would soon be gone.

His kiss slid down the arch of her throat to her collarbone. They were both gasping for breath. "Whatever you were before, you're all woman now."

"Yes." She shuddered and closed her eyes when he bent his head and took her nipple in his mouth. The love games they'd played as teenagers seemed insignificant compared to the heat he was building in her now with the pressure of his teeth and lips. All woman. His woman. She couldn't change that, even if she tried. Tonight he was claiming her body with the natural assurance he'd lacked eight years ago, and she had no defenses against him. But then, she'd probably never had any where Dan was concerned.

When he slid his hands beneath the elastic of her panties, the sensation was the same as if she'd touched a live wire. This was the border beyond which they'd never crossed. They were crossing it now, as Dan knelt before her, drawing the black garment down as his lips and tongue caressed the flat plane of her belly.

Had it been any other man, she would have pulled away in embarrassment as he kissed the damp curls that he slowly uncovered, but she could deny him nothing. Soon any reluctance she felt vanished. He'd found the center of her need for him, and she was aware of nothing but the dizzying pleasure he provided.

When her knees threatened to buckle, he wrapped her in his arms, steadying her while he loved her in a way she'd never known, never allowed before. The hollow ache inside became mind-shattering. She tossed her head from side to side and moaned his name. "Please," she cried. "I want to have . . . all of you."

In answer he swung her into his arms and carried her to the bed. He put her down on top of the spread, not bothering to turn back the covers. She didn't care.

"Love me," she begged, pulling his head down and fitting her mouth to his. She tasted the exotic flavor of her own desire on his lips, and she whimpered with her desperate passion. She fumbled with the studs of his shirt.

Changing their deep kiss to quick, nipping forays, he gradually drew away from her. "Let me take care of that," he said, stilling the frantic movements of her hands. His breathing was rapid and shallow as he worked with the studs, having only slightly better success than she. At last he got them out and wrenched the shirt away. Then he pulled off his shoes and socks and the black satin cummerbund.

When he stood up and stepped out of the dark tuxedo pants, April gazed at him without shame. He was clad only in a pair of tight navy briefs that made his arousal nearly as evident as if he'd had nothing on. "I want you," she whispered. "Come here."

His glance flicked over her, lying naked on the red-and-gold patterned spread, and he shook with the force of his desire. She was so ready for him, skin pink from the friction of his hands and his mouth, and there, where he would sink into the depths of her, the dark curls were damp with passion.

He wanted to strip the briefs from his heated body and bury himself in her now, without waiting. He knew she wouldn't question him if he did. She'd said she wanted impetuosity. Yet he couldn't completely forget his responsibilities. His training ran too deep. "Just a minute," he said softly. "There's something I have to get." He went to the desk and reached into the pocket of his coat.

"Dan?"

He returned to her and leaned down to kiss her swollen lips. "Some things can't be impulsive, April," he murmured. "God, I wish they could."

She reached up and cradled his face in her hands as his meaning became clear. "You're talking about birth control."

"Yes."

"But when..."

"It didn't take me that long just to order wine."

Her eyes filled with tears of chagrin. "Here I blame you for not being spontaneous, and then you save us from...from—"

"Hush, April. Just kiss me."

She did, using every inch of her body, caressing his bare skin as she welcomed the pressure of his hair-sprinkled chest, the hard-muscled leanness of his thighs separating hers. He cupped her bottom in both hands and lifted her to meet his first thrust.

At the moment he entered her, he whispered her name, and she knew she would never forget that urgent, breathless cry. It told her, more than a million spoken words would have, what she needed to know. Whether he admitted the truth or chose to keep silent didn't really matter. He still loved her.

The thought brought her immense joy, followed soon after by a deep, abiding guilt. He still loved her, after all she'd done to make his life miserable. Her frantic desire abated as those eight long years played themselves out in her mind. The memories came between April and her pleasure, draining away the promise of fulfillment.

But Dan deserved more. She wrapped her arms around his sweat-soaked body and moved with him, wanting him to have the completion she couldn't find. When it was over, he might be angry, but for now he'd have the satisfaction he'd waited so long for.

"April," he groaned, "not so...wait, I can't—" He tried to hold her still with the weight of his body.

"It's okay," she whispered, urging him on.

"No. I want—"

"Let go, Dan. Let go."

With a moan that spoke of both ecstasy and despair he gave up his fight for control in an explosive climax. Slowly he sank against her, his body trembling with the aftershock. She held him close and savored her own elation that he'd had this, at least. Now he'd probably leave her, and that would be the end. Men didn't care for women who couldn't respond instantly. Jimmy had taught her that. She waited sadly for his first words.

His labored breathing gradually returned to normal. "Oh, April," he murmured, nuzzling behind her ear. "Next time will be better, especially if you can hold still once in a while. Don't give up on me."

"What do you mean? It's not your fault. I was the one who—"

"Yes, but if I'd had more control, everything might have been different. I was afraid this would happen, after all these years, but have patience. We'll get it right."

"But . . . how do you know? Maybe that's just the way I am. Maybe I'm not any good at this."

His soft laughter rocked them both.

"What's so funny?"

He raised himself on one elbow and gazed down at her with a broad smile. "You. I realize what probably happened. Somewhere along the way you started thinking again, that's all. I warned you about that."

April began to relax. Here was a man who was so secure that he wasn't going to blame her if the experience wasn't everything it could be. What a miracle. He didn't consider her a disappointment. He even seemed to understand. "I did start to think," she admitted. "About how I'd loused things up and never gave us a chance."

Dan's voice and gaze caressed her. "We have that chance now. Unless you're going to spend all your time thinking, that is." He stroked the hair back from her forehead and kissed her there. Then he began lightly rubbing her shoulder and arm in an almost nonsexual way, making no attempt to touch the more sensitive area of her breasts.

As her nervous tension over their first encounter subsided, April felt the warmth of renewed desire prickle her skin. She caught her lip between her teeth and glanced up at him.

"Oh, April, I like the look in those big brown eyes."

"Dan, I—"

"Keep that thought." Gently he levered himself away from her. "I'll be right back."

While he was gone, April recalled the rhythmic excitement as he had moved within her, the urgent force of his thrusting body and the beautiful moment of his climax. This time she vowed to experience that with him, to be a total participant in their lovemaking instead of an observer.

Swinging her legs over the side of the bed, she stood up. Then she threw back the covers and stretched out on the cool white sheets. She moved her hips restlessly and enjoyed the heat created by the friction of the sheet against her skin. Her nipples tightened into hard buds as she remembered the sensation of Dan's lips and teeth closing around them. Yes, he knew how to love her, if she'd let him. And she would let him.

She turned her head on the goose-down pillow and found him standing beside the bed gazing at her. Silently she held out her hand. Grasping it, he lay down beside her, his blue eyes intent on her face.

April licked her dry lips. "I think this time will be different."

"That's nice."

"I want to touch you."

"That would be even nicer."

Slowly she moved her hand downward over his belly until her fingers closed over the velvet shaft that could give her such pleasure if she put aside her guilt and regret over what was past. She closed her eyes and caressed him. His skin was so smooth there, so tight with desire, desire for her. The drenching force of her own passion built as she stroked him.

He moaned and she opened her eyes. She watched with growing excitement as his eyes glazed with passion and his jaw clenched with the force of his attempt at restraint. His need fueled hers, and she began to shake.

"Now," she whispered.

He nodded, unable to speak. He turned away for a moment and then was back, hovering above her. She grasped his hips and pulled him down, down into the moist depths of her innermost self. She was centered there, waiting for him. All else had disappeared. Nothing remained but this joining; nothing mattered but the jolt of feeling every time he pushed forward, the spiraling tension that once had led nowhere and now had a destination.

Inarticulate cries splintered the silence as he brought her closer, ever closer to release. Their bodies became slippery with desire, their muscles as tight as coiled springs. They surged together again and again, each time shuddering in reaction.

With April's last rational moment she called his name before the world became a whirling carnival ride ablaze with lights and color such as she'd never known before. Dimly through the turmoil buffeting her she felt his strong arms around her and his whispered words of love before he joined her in a wild jubilation of fulfillment.

She had no idea how long they lay together in total abandonment. It could have been minutes or hours before Dan left the bed briefly and then returned to lie beside her.

She touched his cheek. "Thank you."

"You did it, not me."

"I'm not so sure. Anyway, you gave me a second chance."

"What fool wouldn't?"

"Dan, all men aren't as sensitive as you are. I learned that lesson the hard way."

He gazed at her thoughtfully. "I'd say old Jimmy has a lot to answer for, after all."

"He was young, too." April traced the fullness of Dan's bottom lip. "Maybe this has all worked out for the best."

"At this particular moment you won't get any arguments from me on that."

"Maybe we weren't ready for each other eight years ago."

"And now?"

She realized how quickly the conversation had turned to the subject of commitment, and this was only the first day of her Chicago visit. Was she in any shape to comment on their relationship, after he'd just given her the most wonderful lovemaking experience of her life? If he asked her to marry him, she'd probably say yes. If he asked her to jump from the top of the John Hancock Center, she'd probably do that, too.

"Let's enjoy this week," she said, smiling to take the sting out of her words, "without thinking about the future just yet. Do you mind?"

A shadow darkened his blue eyes. "Of course not," he said, but his tone betrayed the lie in his words.

"Dan, I've hurt your feelings."

"No." He sighed. "Well, a little. But you're right. I guess now that I've found you again, I want to wrap everything up in a neat little package. That's my personality, you know."

"I know." She tried to laugh but didn't quite make it. The sound was more like a cough. Practical Dan. What she really wanted, she realized, was a romantic courtship in which he wooed her as if he had some doubt about the outcome. As Jimmy had done, perhaps? But that had been such a mess. Still, she wanted more than an easy slipping into the old ways, in which he took their pairing for granted.

Yet she loved the tender way Dan cared for her, and that was part of his personality, too. Was she asking too much to have both in one man, this man?

## 7

DAN LEFT APRIL'S BED in the early hours of the morning and fumbled with his clothes.

Sleepily she rolled to one side and watched him dress. "I wish you didn't have to go."

"Me, too." He bent to give her a quick kiss before tucking in his shirt. "But hardly anyone wears a tux to work at Adonis Sporting Goods."

"Will you have to put in a whole day?"

"Not if I can help it. With any luck I can take the afternoon off, buy you lunch and tour some art galleries afterward."

"That's not necessary. You should probably sleep instead. I'm lousing up your schedule, Dan." She remembered how scrupulous he'd been about keeping training hours when he was a football player.

"Are you kidding?" He sat beside her on the bed and smoothed her hair.

"No. I remember how you used to be about getting your eight hours. I'd stay up all night studying for some test, but not you. You always said sleep was the most important thing, that you couldn't function without it."

He looked down at her and shook his head. "That sounds like me, all right. I even thought about those wonderful sleep requirements of mine when I knew you would be here for five days."

"See? And now it's—" she raised herself on one elbow and looked at the red numbers glowing from the digital clock by the bed "—three-twenty. You'll be lucky to get four hours now."

He smiled. "Three. Unless I skip my morning work-out."

"I feel terrible."

"You should." As he leaned down and nuzzled her ear-lobe, he breathed in the shampoo-fresh scent of her hair. In high school the smell of her hair used to drive him wild. Used to? At this very moment he was wondering if he might be able to stay another hour and still make it to work in some sort of shape.

He couldn't remember ever being this obsessive about a woman. Besides, of all the women in the world this was the one he should avoid. Her track record was terrible with regard to stomping all over his feelings. Yet his appetite for her was insatiable, and he wanted to make the most of every minute she was in Chicago.

"Dan." She grasped his head in both hands and forced him to look at her. "Go home."

"I don't want to. For some reason, sleep has lost all its appeal."

"You'll hate me today while you're propped in your desk chair trying to stay awake, or worse, calling on some client and dozing off in the middle of your sales pitch."

"I doubt I'll hate you, April. Maybe I should just quit my job. It's getting in the way."

She laughed. "Such talk."

"I'm half-serious. Anyway, let's organize this whole thing better."

"Now that's the Dan I know."

"Move to my apartment for the rest of your stay."

She raised both eyebrows.

"Don't worry. Nobody from Booneville has to know about it. You've seen the inside of the Palmer House, so you can describe the room perfectly to Mabel Goodpasture or Bess Easley."

"How did you know what I was thinking? Or that I'd have to describe anything to those two?"

"I also grew up in Booneville, don't forget."

"Well, you're right that I must be able to discuss the decor of my fabulous room, as much to give them a vicarious experience as to prove I stayed here and not with you. But, Dan, I really didn't intend for us to—"

"Live together?"

"I guess that's the expression."

"We're talking about four days, April, not a lifetime." He realized as he said the words that he wasn't talking about four days at all. But he'd settle for that right now. He'd settle for a diet of bread and water and rags to wear if he could have her in his own bed for one more night, let alone four.

"I . . . when would you want me to check out of here? I don't think three-thirty in the morning is exactly—"

His heart began to pound with excitement. She was considering his offer. "Of course it isn't. I'm the only one who has to go rushing off into the night. You can leave later today, say around noon, the normal checkout time. Sleep in this morning. Order breakfast, and pack. I'll pick you up for lunch and the gallery tour, and then we'll head back to my place. How's that?"

"Unfair. You'll be slaving away all morning and squiring me around all afternoon while I play the Queen of Sheba."

"You can make it up to me later."

"I doubt it. You'll be too exhausted."

He gazed into the limitless depths of her brown eyes. "Somehow I don't think so. Have we got a deal?"

"What if you can't get the afternoon off? I'll be checked out with nowhere to go, and I hardly think I'll traipse over to your apartment by myself."

He decided the fencing was over and spoke with firm authority. "I'll get the afternoon off. I'll be in the lobby at twelve to pick you up."

Her capitulation was immediate. "Okay."

Dan took a deep breath. She was his for the next four days.

APRIL WAS SITTING in the lobby, her well-worn suitcase by her side, when Dan walked through the revolving door precisely at noon. The sight of him infected her with the same excitement she used to feel as a child each time she came downstairs on Christmas morning. The expression on his face reflected the same sort of emotion, and April wondered if they were goners, both of them.

She'd stayed awake thinking of him long after he'd left this morning, and even when she'd closed her eyes, his blue gaze had haunted her fretful dreams. It occurred to her that she might be falling in love, but she didn't quite trust her judgment on that score.

She loved how he loved her, but what about the rest, the daily routine of living? April wasn't sure how they'd get along, considering his basically conservative nature. The next four days should be very interesting.

But the next four nights would be more than interesting, she thought as he strode toward her. How typical of him to remember birth control last night, when she'd forgotten completely about that little detail. It wasn't such a little detail, either. Neither of them were in a position to deal with an unplanned pregnancy.

She stood up, wondering what to say as he drew near. Everything was so different between them now. As he approached and she looked into his eyes, her nipples tightened and she felt a fluttering awareness at the apex of her thighs. No one had ever affected her that way with a mere glance, not even Dan eight years ago. But he wasn't quite the same man, and after last night she wasn't at all the same woman. Words of greeting lodged in her throat.

For a moment he didn't speak, either, as they silently assessed each other in the light of day, with all their clothes on and only a few short hours separating them from their last passionate embrace.

Dan cleared his throat. "How're your feet?"

"My feet? Oh—" She looked down at them in surprise. Her feet weren't the part of her clamoring for attention right now, and she'd forgotten about their pivotal role in last night's chain of events. "They're fine as long as I have on these flat shoes, but that's all I can stand to wear."

He coughed into his fist. "Don't I wish."

She looked up at him, startled, and then they both started to laugh. "Lecher," she said under her breath so that only he could hear. It excited her to know he was thinking the same thoughts as she.

"So I'm discovering."

"At least you're a punctual one. It's exactly twelve. You're right on time, as usual."

"So are you, I might point out," he said, gathering her close against his unbuttoned coat. "I've missed you."

He carried the scent of the cold, fresh wind blowing in from the lake, and when she stood on tiptoe to kiss his cheek, his skin was cool. "I've missed you, too."

He drew back with a wry grin. "Not much, judging from that sisterly peck on the cheek. Although I have taken note of the fact you're wearing your contacts, and we all know what that means. Come on, can't you give me a better welcome?"

"Dan, we're in the middle of a hotel lobby."

"That's right. I keep forgetting that you're not used to this big anonymous city. Believe me, April, you won't start any gossip if you give me a decent kiss."

She needed no more encouragement, with his lips so intriguingly close and the memory of last night as fresh as morning coffee. Winding her arms around his neck, she kissed him fully on the mouth.

With a muffled groan he tightened his grip around her waist, and she could feel his heart thudding as they pressed together in full view of hotel clerks and bellhops. Within seconds April forgot everything except the erotic thrust of Dan's tongue as he reminded her eloquently of their last encounter.

Slowly he released her. "Much better," he said, struggling to bring his breathing back to normal. "Too good, in fact. Maybe you knew what you were doing with that peck on the cheek."

April flushed. "Everything's taken care of at the desk. Let's get out of here."

"That means you paid," Dan said, helping her on with her coat. "I had planned to do that. Should have gotten here early, I guess."

"I settled the bill at eleven, in case you tried to. No, Dan. I can manage the expense, especially considering you'll be putting me up for the next four nights."

Dan grinned at her. "That sounds so platonic after the way you just kissed me." He circled her shoulders with one arm and picked up her suitcase. "Let's go."

"By the way, we didn't discuss my truck. Should I follow you this afternoon?" She winced at the idea of trying to drive in tandem through downtown traffic.

He glanced at her. "That wouldn't be much fun. Wait here a second." He put down her suitcase and crossed the lobby.

April watched him talking with the people at the registration desk. When he reached into his back pocket for his wallet, she realized he must be paying for her parking spot for the extra days, and she decided to let him do it. Driving in Chicago wasn't her idea of a good time, and she'd be just as happy to leave the truck parked here until she left town on Friday. Friday. At this moment she didn't want the day ever to arrive.

"Now we can go," Dan said as he returned and hoisted her suitcase once more. "The truck will be fine here until you go home." He took her hand and started toward the revolving door.

"Thank you. I just cost you some money, but I appreciate not having to deal with the traffic."

"It wouldn't have made sense. This is easier, and besides, I want you with me." He proved his point by crowding both of them and the suitcase into one glassed-in section of the revolving door.

April was laughing by the time the spinning door thrust them both outside next to the uniformed doorman. Dan certainly surprised her with these little moments of craziness. Had he been like that before? She didn't think so. Hope rose in her that maybe she and Dan might have a future, after all.

The parking valet arrived with Dan's red Honda and helped April inside while Dan took care of the tip. She admitted reluctantly to herself that she liked being taken care of every once in a while. In her bitterness over Dan's practical handling of their young love eight years ago, she'd shoved aside her memories of his kind consideration and efficient management of details. Now, after the years with Jimmy, she understood how abrasive life could be when a man lacked those skills.

Dan veered into the stream of cars and delivery vans with the ease of a practiced big-city dweller. "We'll eat at a little German place I know—not too fancy but excellent food."

"I'm glad it's not fancy, with me in my sensible shoes." April relaxed as she watched him move deftly around other vehicles. "I haven't asked you anything about where you live. I hope I won't be crowding you."

He gave her a meaningful glance. "No, April, you won't be crowding me."

"How do you know? Have you ever . . . that is, did you have anyone living with you before?"

"No, I never quite trusted anyone enough for that."

She was taken aback. "Because of me?" she ventured.

"Maybe."

"Then why are you having anything to do with me now? Aren't you afraid I'll hurt you all over again?" April herself was afraid of that very thing.

He kept his eyes on the bumper-to-bumper line of cars. "I'm petrified, but I can't stop myself. I should probably have my head examined for getting involved with you, but here I am, delirious with happiness because we'll be together for a few days."

"You are? Deliriously happy?"

"Yes." He stopped at a red light and muttered something she couldn't quite hear.

"What did you say?"

"Oh, nothing. Silly superstition. My mother predicted that having the ring would change my life."

"You mean the heirloom?"

"That's the one."

"Then you don't believe what your mother says about the ring." She felt a familiar twinge of disappointment. He was rejecting a romantic notion once more.

"If it has such power, why didn't it save my father so my mother could grow old with the man she loved?"

"I heard the ring was supposed to bring love to its owners, not guarantee long life. Your parents were very much in love, according to everyone in Booneville."

"And now she's alone."

"With some beautiful memories," April added.

Dan glanced at her. "Maybe that's all the ring is good for, then, beautiful memories."

She knew he was testing her, taunting her to suggest that their relationship might become more than this short interlude, this handful of beautiful memories. Dan liked a sure thing. He always had. But she knew their future together was a long way from a sure thing. She didn't respond to his statement.

She was becoming more and more curious about the ring, however. She couldn't credit it with bringing her and Dan together after eight years. Irene had done that with her clever bequest to the town tied with all sorts of strings designed to snare April and Dan, as well as challenge the townspeople to earn their legacy.

Yet Dan could have resisted the idea of spending time with April and foiled Irene's attempts at matchmaking. Instead, he was pursuing the woman who had hurt him before, and for reasons that seemed to elude him he was risking more heartbreak. Was the ring responsible for that?

Dan stopped for another light, and she gazed at the row of display windows on her side of the street. The tide of lunchtime pedestrians, whipped by the November wind, ebbed and flowed in front of glassed-in mannequins dressed in furs and elegant evening wear. April figured that if she rounded up all the people in this square-block area, she'd have approximately the population of Booneville.

As Dan eased the Honda forward again, April clutched his sleeve. "There! I just saw it!"

"What?"

She craned her neck to keep the small sculpture in view as the current of traffic took them away. "Can you stop?"

"Not here. I'd have to find a parking garage. What did you see?"

"The most beautiful sculpture. I have to know the artist. Please, let's park the car and go back."

"That's a tall order. Besides, what about your feet?"

"Never mind my feet. Look, the next light just turned red. If you can't find a parking garage, drive around the block and pick me up in front of the gallery. I think it had a name like Anderson's or something." Without waiting for an answer she opened the car door and stepped out.

"April . . ."

She glanced back briefly and noticed his exasperated expression. Well, too bad. Chicago was a big city, and she wasn't sure about the name of the gallery. They might not find it again, or if they did, the sculpture might be gone. Besides, excitement drove her to act immediately. She had seen material proof that someone would understand her vision of the sculpture to be placed on the Booneville square.

She dodged honking cars and trucks as she hurried to the safety of the sidewalk. The blisters on her feet hurt, but she ignored the pain and walked quickly down the block. The gallery was somewhere in the middle of the next one, and she had to be in and out with her information before Dan circled back to pick her up. Something about his expression had told her that he wouldn't park the car.

On the second block April moved closer to the stores lining the sidewalk. She caught a glimpse of herself in the reflecting glass and decided she looked a little wild, with her hair blown into disarray and her almost running gait. Dan probably preferred his women to be more sedate. Too bad, again.

The sculpture appeared almost as a surprise in the very next window, and she'd been right about the name of the place, she noticed with satisfaction. She stood very close to the window and looked.

The sculpture stood about two feet high and was the color of dry earth. April cocked her head to each side, trying to determine if the shape was anything recognizable, but she finally decided it was not, unless it mimicked something as free-form as a piece of driftwood. All the movement of the piece as it undulated and intertwined was upward, reaching, stretching toward some indefinable goal.

The title of the sculpture was printed on a small card propped next to it. April laughed when she read the title. How appropriate to everything that had happened to her and was still happening. The name of the sculptor was Erica Jorgenson, and the piece cost three hundred and fifty dollars.

April opened the wooden gallery door and stepped inside. She was the only person in the small area except for a blond man who approached eagerly at her entrance.

"Can I help you?"

"Yes. I need two things," April said, surveying the paintings and sculpture arranged around the room. She liked the simple, fresh quality evidenced in everything on display, but nothing moved her like the piece in the window. "First of all, I must contact Erica Jorgenson about commissioning her for some work."

The man nodded. "That can be arranged. I'll need a phone number for you."

April found her wallet and extracted the card that Dan had given her with both of his telephone numbers on it. She gave out the one for his apartment and hoped he wouldn't object. Anyway, hadn't her move there been his idea?

"And what is your second request?" the man asked as he wrote down Dan's number on a pad of paper.

"I'd like to buy that piece of Ms Jorgenson's that you have in the window."

"Of course."

Of course. April smiled at his nonchalance while she wrote out the check. This gallery owner had no idea that she didn't do this every day, or that she'd have to sell a heck of a lot of eggs to pay for something that wouldn't feed the chickens or harvest the apples or weed the vegetable garden. But she believed what she'd told the board members, that the human spirit sometimes needs to view something that has no other purpose except beauty.

He wrapped the sculpture in bubbled plastic and boxed it while April watched out the window for Dan's red Honda. She hated to see the sculpture disappear because she wanted to show it to him right away. Now she would have to wait until later, probably until they got to his apartment, before she could unwrap it.

The red Honda appeared from the left and pulled up next to the curb in a no-parking zone. April figured Dan hated doing that, and she fidgeted impatiently while the gallery owner taped the box shut. Then she mumbled her thanks and headed quickly out the door.

Dan leaned over and swung the car door open for her. "I thought you went in for information," he said, eyeing the box.

"I bought the sculpture." Horns honked all around them, but April took the time to settle the box in the back of the Honda before climbing in so that Dan could pull away from the curb.

"You bought it? Isn't that a little small for the town square?"

April laughed. "I bought it for me. I sure hope Erica Jorgenson will do the sculpture for the square, though. Her work is everything I dreamed of. I can imagine something very similar to this, although perhaps in a different medium, maybe bronze."

"What's it of?"

"Well, um . . ." April thought of how to describe her purchase and how Dan might react to her vague description. "Maybe I should wait and let you see it rather than trying to picture it for you."

He shrugged. "Okay. Ready to eat?"

"Sure."

Throughout their hearty lunch in a little basement restaurant famous for good German food and imported beer, April tried to put aside her thoughts about the sculpture she'd bought and the woman who had created it. By now the gallery owner might have relayed April's message, and Dan's phone could be ringing.

"Do you have an answering machine at your apartment?" she asked Dan abruptly as they finished off their apple strudel.

"Yes. Why?"

"I hope you don't mind, but the gallery owner asked for a number where the sculptor could call me, and I gave him yours. I'm glad you have an answering machine so that I won't miss her call."

"*Her* call?"

"Erica Jorgenson, the sculptor."

"Oh. A woman, huh?"

"Women sculpt, too, you know."

"I'm aware of that, but don't you think hiring a woman might be asking for trouble in Booneville? You've already got an uphill battle with people like Henry Goodpasture."

"Who is sexist. I hope you're not, Dan."

"I do my damnedest to avoid it, but I wasn't exactly raised in the bosom of liberal thinking. If my grandmother hadn't been around, I'd be worse off than I am."

"Dan, I have a special feeling about this sculptor. I wouldn't care if the piece I bought was created by an orangutan. I'd still want that artist to design something for the town square."

"Does that mean we can forget the gallery tour this afternoon? Maybe this situation has merit, after all."

April taunted him with a smile. "Getting tired? And you were the one who insisted that wouldn't happen."

"I said I wouldn't be tired. I didn't say I wouldn't want to go to bed," Dan said, leaning his chin on one hand to gaze at her.

"Dan, my goodness."

"Your goodness is right. And your sweetness, and your loveliness, and your sexiness. I want all of those things. Let's skip the galleries."

Her pulse quickened at the light in his eyes. "I'm worried that the board might not think I've checked enough places."

"But from the way you're talking, your mind is made up."

"I think it is, yes. Except that you're supposed to be—what was the word?—supervising me."

A lazy smile spread across his lips. "Yeah. I plan to do that a lot."

"Dan, be serious. What will we tell the board?"

"As little as possible," he replied with a grin.

"I know how we'll do this. I'll unwrap—"

"Good beginning."

She glared at him. "I'll unwrap the sculpture when we get home, and if you approve, I'll pursue hiring Erica Jorgenson, assuming she'll work for the paltry sum we have to offer. If you don't approve, I'll look for some other possibilities in the next three days." April mentally crossed her fingers. What if he didn't like the piece she had just bought? Then she'd deal with that when it happened, she told herself sternly. Irene used to warn her not to buy trouble.

"That means we can head home right now, doesn't it?"

"I guess so, unless you want me to get the sculpture out of the car and unwrap it here."

"Not on your life. I prefer my unveiling ceremonies to take place in private."

He whisked her out of the restaurant and back to the car in record time, and within minutes they entered the underground garage beneath his apartment building. An elevator took them, along with her suitcase and the boxed sculpture, to the fourth floor.

"I wish I could dazzle you with the penthouse," he said as they stepped into a carpeted hallway, "but the rent goes up with every floor."

Now that they were in his apartment building, April was taut with the anticipation of being in his arms once more. "Who cares about a view?" she said, casting him a provocative look.

"There's only one view *I'm* interested in right now." He took his keys from his pocket as they approached his door.

"My sculpture," she teased, lifting the box she carried.

"Right." He turned the key in the lock. "Hey, do we have to look at this thing right now?"

"Yes. I really want you to see it."

"Damn, that's too bad." He shook his head and ushered her inside.

His apartment, she could tell in that first instant when she stepped into the living room, was immaculate. And although the color scheme in shades of brown didn't show much imagination, the furniture had the sort of free-flowing, Scandinavian elegance she'd always admired. With a touch of bright color here and there the room could be saved from its present air of sterility. He even had a small fireplace, although it looked as if it had never seen a burning log.

"Very nice, Dan." April set the box containing the sculpture on the coffee table and turned to him with a smile.

He put down her suitcase and gazed at her with his hands shoved into the pockets of his coat.

"Dan? Is something wrong?"

"No. I just . . . never thought you'd be standing here, that's all. I'm— It takes some getting used to."

She gazed back at him. "I never thought I'd be standing here, either. I figured after all that had happened, there was no way we'd ever be together again. I'm glad we are."

"Me, too."

They stood silently for a moment longer, each of them absorbing the emotions flowing between them. At last April spoke softly. "I'll unpack the sculpture, and then . . ."

Dan snapped out of his reverie. "By all means, unpack that sculpture if we have to take care of that first. I'll hang up our coats and see if I can find us a bottle of wine in the refrigerator."

"Would you please check your phone messages, too?"

"Sure thing."

After he left with their coats, April stripped the tape from the box and lifted out the wrapped sculpture. By the time he returned with a chilled green bottle and two wine-glasses, she had positioned the smooth piece of art in the center of the coffee table and was standing back to admire it.

Dan stopped and stared. "*That's* what you plan to erect on the Booneville town square?"

"Yes." She was so lost in contemplation of her new ac-quisition that she didn't notice the dismay in his tone. "Or something close. It will be spectacular, don't you think?"

Dan closed his eyes. "I think," he began slowly, open-ing his eyes again, "that it will be a disaster."

"What?" Stung by his reaction, she whirled to face him.

"It won't work."

"Don't say that! I don't want to hear that, especially from you!"

"Okay, I won't say it." He walked toward the coffee ta-ble. "Does this have a name?"

"Yes." She folded her arms and glared at him through sudden tears. Dammit. Dammit to hell.

"What's it called?"

She hurled the answer like a javelin. "*Impulse*."

# 8

DAN'S TONE BECAME SOFT, careful, as if he were in the presence of a ticking bomb. "What are you trying to do, April?"

"Bring some beauty to the Booneville square." She fought her tears. She would convince him that the sculpture was a good idea, and not by sobbing on his shoulder, either.

"That's too simple an answer, and you know it. How can you imagine something like this, maybe a ten- or fifteen-foot version, in Booneville? Henry Goodpasture expects somebody on a horse."

"I didn't promise Henry that."

"But you didn't mention what you really wanted, either."

"They wouldn't have reacted well to some garbled description of mine. They'll have to see something, something like this."

"And when they do, I predict the whole project will be canned before it gets started."

"No! I'll bet M.G. Tucker will like the sculpture, and I do, and Bill might be persuaded. That's three out of six. So if you . . ." She didn't finish the sentence. Judging from the expression on his face, he was way ahead of her.

"I'm the swing vote."

"Dan, let me explain what I—"

"That's okay. I think I get it now. You zeroed in on this sculpture in the gallery window, knew it was the type of stuff you wanted, and without further discussion you want rubber-stamp approval from me. That would help you convince M.G. and Bill to go along, wouldn't it?"

"I thought you'd agree that the sculpture is beautiful, Dan. It's graceful, imaginative, unique—"

"That's a good word—unique."

"What about your Scandinavian decor in here?" she continued, flinging out her arms. "I would have said you'd love something like this after seeing the furniture you've chosen."

"Wait a minute. I never said I wouldn't consider it for this room. Maybe I would. But we're talking about the town square, not my apartment."

"And everything must have its appropriate time and place." April glared at him. "I've heard that somewhere before. About eight years ago, to be exact."

"April, dammit!" He crossed to her and took her by the shoulders. "Do you enjoy being unreasonable? Why must you always go against the grain?"

She gasped in surprise at his aggressive tone and the forceful grip that brought them into close contact. Years before he would have retreated into injured silence at her taunts, but now he was challenging her, physically and mentally. Both anger and passion flared in his blue eyes.

April fought her attraction to that potent combination. She was determined to hold her ground. "Maybe I go against the grain because that's the only way to keep life from stagnating."

"Then what the hell are you doing in Booneville? You're not making sense. If your biggest worry is stagnation, I can't imagine why you'd choose to live in a conservative Midwestern town where you run the greatest risk of doing the very thing you fear most."

"Maybe that's part of the challenge." Her heart was beating as if she'd run up a flight of stairs. She wanted to win this argument, but she also wanted his lips on hers. He was so close she could smell the clean scent of his skin mixed with the musty fragrance of arousal.

"And to think I believed your little speech about being a small-town girl at heart."

"But I am. Don't you see?"

"No, I don't." His gaze dropped to her mouth for a brief moment. Then with an impatient shake of his head he looked into her eyes once more. "Explain it to me."

April took a steadying breath. "Small towns are warm, cozy places to live in. They're also in danger of sinking into a rut. But I can fix that."

"With this sculpture?"

"Yes."

He stared at her in frustration. "You're asking for trouble."

"Maybe."

He gripped her more tightly. "I think you *are* trouble."

Her body was quivering with need for him, but she lifted her chin defiantly. "What do you plan to do about that, Dan?"

His voice was low. "Right now?" He slid one hand behind her head to hold it still. "What I should have done when we walked into this apartment."

She trembled as he brought his mouth deliberately closer, and when their lips met, she moaned softly. He kissed her with firm mastery, draining away her anger and his, replacing it with churning need.

At last he lifted his head and spoke with difficulty. "We'll . . . work everything out later."

Dazed with the force of his kiss, she nodded.

"Come here." He led her toward the couch and drew her down, facing him. Slowly he traced a line with his finger from the hollow of her throat to the top button of her blouse. "Undress for me, April."

She gazed at him and knew that she had no business being here. But last night wasn't easily forgotten. She wanted more, no matter how unwise her longing might be. "All right." In the afternoon light she studied the face that had hovered over her during their spiraling moments of passion. The faint shadow of his dark beard was beginning to show along his jawline and upper lip and in the hard-to-shave cleft of his chin. She was filled with excitement at the thought of loving him here in the full light of day, surrounded by the order of his neat-as-a-pin living room.

Dan leaned against the back of the sofa and rested his arm along the top of the cushions. He didn't touch her, but his blue eyes burned with intensity.

She crossed her legs at the knee, and her nylons slid against each other with a faint whispering sound. The ache for him grew inside her, blocking out rational thought and inspiring her to tease him, tempt him into disrupting this proper setting with their wild need for each other.

Dan stared at the spot where her skirt fell gracefully over her knee but had crept up on one side to reveal a sleek strip of thigh. April adjusted her skirt a little higher yet. With calm purpose she unfastened the first button of her blouse. He swallowed as she moved to the next button.

"Am I doing this right?" she murmured, unfastening another button.

"There's no doing it wrong."

When all the buttons were undone, she slipped the blouse from her shoulders and reached one hand behind her back to unhook her bra. As she let it fall away, baring herself to his gaze, his face contorted with desire. With a moan he reached for her and pressed his face against her breasts.

She held his head as he nipped and nibbled at her heated flesh in a near frenzy to taste her, to suck the hard buds she thrust toward him. "I'm . . . not finished," she said, gasping.

He pressed her back onto the soft cushions. "I don't care." His breath was hot against her breasts. "I've got to have you now."

She arched against the pressure of his mouth as he stoked the fire within her. Sliding his hand up her thigh, he found the waistband of her panty hose. With her help he tugged that garment and her panties away and tossed them to the floor.

Pushing aside her skirt, he pressed the palm of his hand against her. "God, you're so wet," he whispered, stroking her.

She moaned in response. How glorious to be aroused like this, to want someone so much that she had no shame. She lifted her hips toward the magic he was working and begged him to love her.

Dimly she realized there must be one more step before that could happen, but he had taken care of everything before. When he fumbled with the catch of his slacks, she realized, even through the dizzying haze of passion, that he wouldn't take care of everything this time. For perhaps the first moment in his life he'd abandoned reason, just as she'd once wished he would do. Did that make reason her task? "Dan, wait."

"No."

"Get something first. You really don't want . . ."

His chest heaved as he struggled for the breath to speak. "That's not quite right. *You* don't want."

*"We* don't want."

"Wrong." He kissed her almost savagely and lurched to his feet. "But I'm a good guy. I'll be right back."

When he returned, some of the frenzy was gone. She knew it was wrong to regret that it was. When he entered her, he was in control again, moving skillfully inside her, turning the tables and bringing her to heights of mindless ecstasy. Deliberately he wrung from her the cries of release before he allowed his own needs to carry him beyond the bounds of his control.

They lay sprawled on the sofa as daylight seeped from the room.

"Now we should go to bed," Dan finally murmured against her ear. "To sleep."

"Probably should." She shifted slightly under his weight. "Dan, I'm sorry that I kept you from the . . . full enjoyment of . . ." She was floundering, trying to find the right words.

"I enjoyed myself."

"Yes, but—"

"You did the right thing, April. For one crazy minute there I wanted to make you pregnant. Wasn't that stupid?"

She began to tremble. "You did?" The idea of carrying Dan's baby made her heart swell for a moment.

"Sure. When we were fighting about the sculpture, I wondered if you were about to leave me again. I thought of a desperate and foolish way to keep you around."

"So you weren't beyond reason at all. You knew what you were doing."

"Yes. But I've never had such a wild impulse in my life before, believe me."

She smiled back. "Impulse?"

"Yeah." He smiled back.

"Maybe my sculpture had some effect."

"Maybe. Or that crazy ring. Something's messing with my head."

"Seems like it, Dan." She hesitated to tell him how much his impulse to give her a child thrilled her. "What makes you think my being pregnant would make any difference between us? This is the eighties, you know."

"Instinct, I guess. Would it?"

"Yes, and that's why we're not going to let it happen. If we decide to . . . go on together, in some fashion, there mustn't be anything affecting our decision except ourselves."

"You're right. And that's why we need to get this sculpture business settled and out of the way."

"The sculpture! I completely forgot to ask if you had any calls on your answering machine."

"Just one from Erica Jorgenson, asking you to call as soon as possible," he said lightly.

"What? You should have told me sooner." April struggled to sit up, forcing Dan to roll away from her onto the floor, where he landed with a thump.

"Hey!"

"Gee, I'm sorry." She peered down at him in the dim light. "Are you okay?"

"I think I've just been dumped for a piece of sculpture."

"You're so witty." She ruffled his hair and picked up her discarded blouse as she stepped over his prone body. "Where's the answering machine?"

"In the bedroom," he said, "right down that hall. On the table where the drawer is still pulled out, as I recall. Some guy was in a hurry, and the woman seemed to be in a bit of a hurry herself. Remember that?"

"Oh."

"Yeah, *oh*. Would you rather have made your call first?"

"Don't be silly. Why don't you pour us some wine while I'm gone?"

He watched her go, buttoning her blouse as she left. "I hope I'm not being silly," he said softly to himself.

ERICA WAS DELIGHTED to hear from April, and they agreed to meet at Dan's apartment. After conferring with Dan, April set the time for ten in the morning, following his suggestion that she meet with the sculptor while he was at work. April welcomed the chance to talk with Erica alone, considering Dan's less-than-enthusiastic attitude toward the project.

To his credit, he was attempting to compromise. Although his judgment remained the same, he'd agreed not to block April's attempt to win over the rest of the board. He would remain noncommittal, neither endorsing nor denigrating the modernistic concept, thus giving her time to get a reaction from the other four members and the town in general.

All of this was predicated on Erica's acceptance of the commission, and April had doubts about that, considering the small amount of money the town had to offer. She kept her reservations to herself, however, as she and Dan enjoyed their first breakfast together and discovered the joys of a romp in bed when they were both fresh from a good night's sleep.

After Dan left for work, late for the first time since taking the job, April prepared for Erica's visit by making coffee and setting out a plateful of chocolate-and-marshmallow cookies she found in Dan's cupboard. She chided herself for her down-home preparations. If Erica Jorgenson turned out to be anything like her work, she wouldn't be swayed by coffee and cookies into creating a masterpiece for a pittance. Still, April hoped the sculptor turned out to be exactly like her work.

She wasn't disappointed. Erica arrived in a swirl of royal purple that partially hooded her abundant blond hair and draped in imaginative folds from her lithe body. April estimated that Erica might be close to six feet tall.

"I'm Erica Jorgenson," she said immediately when April opened the door. Then she swept inside without waiting for an invitation.

April became aware that her mouth was open and closed it before she turned around to greet her visitor. Erica had thrown back the purple hood and was standing with her hands on her hips and her legs braced apart while she surveyed the sculpture in the middle of the coffee table. Too late April realized she shouldn't have set the plate of marshmallow cookies and the coffee cups on the same table. The sculpture deserved its own space free of clutter.

"I'll create a pedestal for you," Erica said, unhooking her cape and flinging it onto the couch. "This will never do." Underneath the cape she was dressed in an expensive-looking jumpsuit in winter white that was belted at her hips with an oversize gold chain.

"The sculpture won't stay in this room," April said, and immediately tried to picture where it would fit in her Victorian farmhouse. But wasn't the point to jolt people with a few surprises, a few things out of place? "I'm taking it back to Booneville."

"Where?" Erica focused her gray eyes on April as if seeing her for the first time.

"Booneville, Illinois. It's a very small town, so I'm not surprised you haven't been there."

"I take it you live in Booneville, then?"

"Yes."

"Small towns can be very nice. What do you do there?"

April recognized that Erica was accustomed to making judgments about everything, and she smiled to herself as she answered the question. "I run a poultry and produce farm called The Birds and the Bees." What would Erica say if April suggested the sculpture was purchased to help her hens lay better? Maybe the artist would snatch her work and leave.

To April's surprise, Erica chuckled and gave her a warm look. "Cute name."

"It's not a big farm, but I like it there."

"I can relate to that."

"You can?"

"Sure. I've often thought about moving to the country. The peace and quiet would be heavenly for my work, but I'd have a hell of a time marketing my sculpture in Booneville, Illinois. For that I need the big city."

April grabbed the opportunity to plug Booneville. "I think you'd love spending time downstate, Erica—as a change of pace, of course. Sit down, please, and I'll tell you my plan. Would you care for coffee?"

"Regular or decaf?"

"Regular." April had found both in the cupboard and had chosen the full-strength brew, figuring a cosmopolitan creature like Erica wouldn't mess around with anything less.

"Then I'll pass, thanks." Erica sat down on the sofa as if she owned it. "I have to keep a steady hand for my work."

"Of course." To avoid appearing too chummy, April chose a chair at right angles to the couch. After Erica's response to her offer of coffee, she didn't mention the cookies and wished fervently that she knew a magic trick to make them disappear. Fruit and cheese might have worked, and maybe a glass of Perrier.

To April's dismay, Erica looked directly at the marshmallow-and-chocolate mound squatting pathetically beside her glorious work of art. "These look sinful."

"You're right. I shouldn't have put them out."

"No, you shouldn't have. Here goes my diet." Erica picked up a cookie with obvious relish and bit into it.

April stared at her.

"Well, don't just sit there making me feel guilty. You have to eat them, too."

April grinned. "Would you like some milk?"

"Please."

Within minutes they were both munching away, and Erica was dipping her cookies into her milk. "Now that we're reduced to our real selves," Erica announced as she took a third cookie, "I should probably tell you my real name, which is Bertha Crabapple."

April choked on her milk.

"Please don't spread this information around, April."

"But you look so . . . so *Swedish*."

"I think so, too. Maybe in another life I was Swedish. I've been thinking of changing my name formally, but I haven't done it yet, so occasionally somebody like Rolf Anderson, the gallery owner, will slip and call me Bertha. I thought you should know, if we'll be working together."

"But you don't even know what I want you to do."

"No, but I like your taste." Erica tipped her head toward the sculpture. "And your decisiveness. Rolf mentioned that you barreled into the gallery and bought this in less than five minutes."

"Well, I—"

"Don't explain. You might ruin my fantasy. I love to imagine people are that excited about my work."

"Oh, I absolutely am."

"What is it you want me to create for you, then?"

April outlined her project for the town square and included a description of the gazebo as the counterpoint to a large sculpture created by Erica, a sculpture similar to the one resting in front of them.

Erica nodded, a faraway look in her eyes. "Bringing modern art to the hinterlands. I like it." Then she glanced at April. "Although frankly I'm surprised that your farm is prosperous enough for you to donate such a generous gift to the town. You must have super chickens down there in Booneville."

"Oh, it's not my money. A dear old lady died and left the income from her estate to the town. That's where the funds are coming from."

Some of the enthusiasm left Erica's expression. "Ah. And how much are we talking about?"

April paused. The amount she had to offer seemed to shrink in her mind until it was laughably inadequate. Finally she worked up enough courage to say the figure out loud.

Sure enough, Erica laughed. Then she stood up and reached for her cape. "The cookies were marvelous, and I'll be glad to make you a pedestal for this piece." She gestured toward the sculpture. "But as for the town square, I think we're wasting each other's time."

# 9

"ERICA, WAIT!" April caught up with her before she reached the door. "Isn't there any way? Perhaps you could use less expensive materials, or make the sculpture a little smaller. And we wouldn't have to have it right away. We could wait until you have spare time."

Erica shook her head as she tossed her cape around her shoulders. "You're talking about compromising the integrity of the project, and you don't want that. Better to have nothing than something less than what you envisioned." She gazed with sympathy at April. "Maybe you can find another sculptor who would be willing to do this for the exposure without making anything on it. The amount you're talking about would barely cover the cost of materials."

"I don't want another sculptor. The minute I saw your work in the gallery window I knew you were the one who could create exactly what I had in mind. Now I'll compare every other artist's sculpture with yours and find it wanting."

"I love to hear all of that, of course, but I have to earn a living, too. And besides the materials, I'd have expenses when I came down there to erect the sculpture because I'd have it shipped in pieces. I'd have hotel bills, meals—"

"No, you'd stay with me in the peace and quiet of the country. You could stay as long as you liked, Erica, and work on other things, too. Didn't you mention that you'd enjoy that? Here's your chance."

# IT'S A WILD, WILD, WONDERFUL
# FREE OFFER!

## HERE'S WHAT YOU GET:

**1.** *Four New Harlequin Temptation® Novels—FREE!* Everything comes up hearts and diamonds with four exciting romances — yours FREE from Harlequin Reader Service. Each of these brand-new novels brings you the passion and tenderness of today's greatest love stories.

**2.** *A Useful, Practical Digital Clock/Calendar—FREE!* As a free gift simply to thank you for accepting four free books we'll send you a stylish digital quartz clock/ calendar — a handsome addition to any decor! The changeable, month-at-a-glance calendar pops out, and may be replaced with a favorite photograph.

**3.** *An Exciting Mystery Bonus—FREE!* You'll go wild over this surprise gift. It will win you compliments and score as a splendid addition to your home.

**4.** *Money-Saving Home Delivery!* Join Harlequin Reader Service and enjoy the convenience of previewing four new books every month, delivered to your home. Each book is yours for $2.24—26 cents less per book than what you pay in stores. And there is no extra charge for postage and handling. Great savings and total convenience are the name of the game at Harlequin!

**5.** *Free Newsletter!* It makes you feel like a partner to the world's most popular authors…tells about their upcoming books…even gives you their recipes!

**6.** *More Mystery Gifts Throughout the Year!* No joke! Because home subscribers are our most valued readers, we'll be sending you additional free gifts from time to time—as a token of our appreciation!

# GO WILD
## WITH HARLEQUIN TODAY—
## JUST COMPLETE, DETACH AND
## MAIL YOUR FREE-OFFER CARD!

# IT'S NO JOKE!

MAIL THE POSTPAID CARD AND
GET FREE GIFTS AND $10.00 WORTH OF
HARLEQUIN NOVELS — *FREE!*

"Yes, but—"

"You also mentioned exposure, and that wouldn't hurt, either. I'm sure a project like this would merit all sorts of media coverage, and I'd make sure that you got it." April tried not to think of how the residents of Booneville would react to television cameras on the town square.

"You have a point there, I'll admit. None of us in the art world is successful enough to ignore publicity opportunities, but this would cost me a bundle, and I'm inclined to let someone else have the limelight this time."

April took a deep breath and played her ace. It could be the high card that won the hand or the low one that solidified Erica's refusal. "One thing I didn't mention before was that I expect some resistance to the project from a conservative faction in the town."

"Oh?" Erica raised an eyebrow.

"Some people in Booneville want to keep things exactly as they've always been, no matter how boring that might be. One man in particular, the president of the bank, didn't want a sculpture at all. Finally he agreed that we might have one if it could be a soldier on a horse or something like that."

"I see." The light of battle crept into Erica's gray eyes.

The subtle transformation registered with April and she continued talking. "The woman who died and left money to the town was a good friend of mine and a very creative person. In her will she appointed me, the only woman, to the board that administers the funds. I think she intended that I keep the town moving forward, and this sculpture is my way of striking a blow for progress."

"What about this resistance? Is it strong enough to thwart your plan for my sculpture?"

"I don't know," April answered honestly. She noticed that Erica had said "my sculpture." She was considering the idea. "But I'd put everything into the fight to guarantee that you get the commission and not somebody who's willing to create a soldier on a horse."

Erica faced April for the first time since starting out the door. "I think we have enough military statues in Illinois, don't you?"

"I certainly do."

Erica extended her hand. "You get that bank president to come around, and I'll put up your sculpture."

April felt like shouting but decided to wait until Erica was gone. "Thank you." She accepted Erica's firm handshake with as much dignity as she could muster. "Thank you very much."

Once Erica was out the door and safely down the hall, April let loose with a triumphant yell. Had she been in Booneville, the volume would have summoned every hog for miles around.

HER MISSION COMPLETED, April could have cut her visit short and returned to Booneville. Instead, she ignored logic and chose to stay with Dan until her scheduled departure on Friday morning.

"We organized this wrong," Dan said Thursday night as they lay side by side, hips and shoulders touching, fingers intertwined as they basked in the warm glow of their lovemaking.

April smiled. Dan would probably always think in terms of good or poor organization. That part of him would never change, and that was okay with her. His imaginative and impassioned loving more than made up for a tendency to organize most everything else in his life.

"We should have had you come up over a weekend instead of during the workweek," Dan continued. "Any chance you can stay through Monday morning?"

She turned her head on the pillow and gazed at him. "That sounds nice, but I don't think so."

He rolled to his side and slid his hand around her waist to draw her nearer. "We could sleep in Saturday morning. We'd have all the time in the world for a change, instead of having to watch the clock. I'd even serve you breakfast in bed." He placed a kiss on her breast. "Have you ever had breakfast in bed?"

She turned to mold her body against his. "Depends on your definition of breakfast."

"If you stay with me this weekend, we'll create a whole page of definitions."

"Oh, Dan," she said with a sigh. "I can't." She brushed her lips against the smooth cleft in his chin. Typical of his caring behavior, he'd shaved before he took her to bed. "Mom and Dad have been kind enough to mind the farm and do the chores for five days, but I can't impose on them any longer. They've built quite a little social life for themselves in town, and I know staying out there for the weekend would be a bother. That's one reason I set things up this way."

"That farm really ties you down, April."

She stiffened. "So does your job." She'd been wondering if they'd get to this, and if he'd assume she'd give up the life she'd made for herself to be with him in Chicago. "Do you really enjoy selling sporting goods?"

"Beats farming."

"How about living in Chicago? I asked you once before, and you evaded the question."

"Adonis doesn't have an office in Booneville, and something tells me they aren't likely to open one soon. In fact, the next promotion I'm in line for would mean moving to Cincinnati."

"I see."

"That doesn't mean I'll take it, April. A lot depends on ... what happens."

"Between us," she clarified.

He lifted his head to gaze down at her. "Does this mean anything to you, what we've found together in the past few days?"

"Of course it does."

"Would you like it to continue?"

She regarded him steadily. "On what terms?"

"No terms. Not for now. With what we've just said I realize that it's too soon for either of us to be suggesting major changes in our lives to accommodate this ... feeling between us."

"You're not ready to put a name to it, are you?"

"Are you?"

She stared at him as the tense silence grew. "No," she said softly. "We said those words to each other once before, but I don't think either of us knew what they meant."

"No, we didn't."

"What I felt for you then seems shallow compared to what I feel now, but I don't know if I'm driven by plain old ordinary lust or something more."

He smiled at her. "I wouldn't classify this lust as 'plain old ordinary.' I'd at least give it a rating of colossally wonderful."

She traced the bow of his upper lip. "So would I, come to think of it."

"You know, I do have one term."

"What's that?"

"I want you to keep the ring for a while."

"The ring? Oh, Dan, I don't think—"

"Not to wear. I understand what that would mean to the entire town if they saw it on your finger. But I— Lord, I can't believe what I'm about to say."

"Now I'm really curious."

Dan took a deep breath. "All my life I've heard stories about this ring and how it affects people. I've refused to believe any of it, but . . ."

"You're weakening," she prompted.

"I think so. Ever since my mother gave me the damn thing, you've been an obsession with me. Then this sculpture project came up, and the board asked me to work with you on it. We haven't agreed on that subject, but at least it brought you up here and we've . . . found other areas of agreement."

She lifted her head and kissed him gently. "I'd say so."

"April, I . . ." He gazed into her eyes. "This sounds crazy, but I want to try an experiment. You keep the ring for a few weeks, and let's see what happens."

His seriousness confused her. It wasn't what she expected from Dan, and a vague urge to return to the status quo prompted her to tease him. "If you want a real experiment, you could give it to the cleaning lady and see what happens."

"I don't want the cleaning lady to become obsessed with me."

His response flooded her with surprise followed by tingling warmth. "But you want me to?" she murmured.

"Yes."

APRIL TOOK THE RING HOME on Friday morning. After making love to Dan again in the early light of dawn, she doubted the ring was necessary to keep him uppermost in her thoughts. Still, the very fact that he wanted her to have it was exciting. Whether the ring had special powers or not, Dan was willing to consider the possibility. His new attitude fed April's fantasy that he might possess the romantic streak she longed for in a man.

The ring was to be their secret, so April didn't mention it to her parents when she recounted the details of her trip that afternoon. She also minimized the amount of time she'd spent with Dan and eliminated entirely the information that she'd stayed at his apartment.

She did unearth her sculpture, however, and her parents were speechless for several seconds. At last they mumbled something about the piece being "interesting" and left quickly for their home in town.

April returned to her routine of evening chores and realized that the familiar jobs gave her plenty of time to think about Dan while she worked. As she gathered eggs and tossed scratch corn to her cackling brood, April was astonished to encounter loneliness for the first time in years. She missed Dan.

When darkness covered the farm and the chickens were settled for the night, April wandered back to the house for a solitary meal and an empty evening. Tonight she would not lie in Dan's arms, nor enjoy the gentle caress that transformed her into the passionate woman she was meant to be. The peaceful serenity of a night in the country had become intolerably quiet without the sound of Dan's key in the lock, his eager greeting, his murmured words of pleasure as she held him close after the long hours of separation.

Turning on lights as she went, she walked into her bedroom and took the ring out of her top dresser drawer. The gold setting was the deep yellow of very old jewelry, and for the first time April examined the faint crest etched inside the ring behind the setting.

The crest was divided down the middle and engraved with a jagged mountain peak on the left and three stars on the right. Something was written in tiny script beneath the crest. April adjusted her glasses and held the ring to the light. Just under the crest was a French-sounding name, Montclair, and centered below that was some sort of inscription.

When April realized the words were French and not English, she figured them out. The inscription read:

A.
avec amour,
C.

A thrill of romantic pleasure ran through her. The woman originally given this ring had the same first initial as April's. She wondered if the woman and her lover had indeed lived in France and had once been part of the French nobility.

She felt a sense of privilege in having the ring, even temporarily. Hesitantly she slipped it on her finger. It fit. She turned it to catch the rainbow of light that sparkled from the diamonds ringing the teardrop-shaped emerald.

Stretching her hand in front of her, she wondered how such an elegant ring could feel so natural on the finger of an Illinois farm girl. As the cool metal warmed to the temperature of her skin, April's thoughts strayed to Dan. She pictured him putting the ring on her finger in front of a congregation of friends and family. With a shiver of delight she imagined his deep voice pledging to love her forever.

The telephone jangled in the next room, one long and one short ring—her line. Without taking the heirloom jewelry from her finger April went to the kitchen and picked up the receiver.

"I miss you so much I'm going crazy."

"Dan! I can't believe it's you. The ring—I put it on a few minutes ago, and here you are calling me."

"If it was working the way I'd hoped, you'd be calling me."

"Another few minutes and I might have."

"What were you thinking about?"

"You. I said that."

"I want details."

"Dan, this is a party line. Someone could pick up the phone at any minute and—"

"Okay, then talk in code. I'll understand."

April cleared her throat. "That's not necessary. They were general thoughts, really. I miss you, too."

"You're evading the issue, but I won't push it. And I hope to hell you miss me."

"I do, and watch your language. If someone picks up the phone, I want you to start talking about your grandmother's will or something, okay?"

"Okay." He paused. "How are you doing, really?"

"Not great. Once you asked me if I was lonely on the farm all by myself, and I said no. But tonight, for the first time, I am."

"Damn, I want to be with you. Whoops, sorry. Anyway, I've tried to figure out an excuse to come down and see you that wouldn't set everyone's tongue wagging."

"It wouldn't work. They're already speculating about how well we got along in Chicago, I imagine. I told my mother and father an edited version of my visit that they didn't seem to swallow completely. They're at a potluck supper this very minute, and I'm sure you and I are the major topic of conversation."

"Did you show them the sculpture?"

"Uh-huh."

"And?"

"They were struck dumb."

"Hmm."

"And then they said it was 'interesting.' I don't think they loved it, but then, I didn't expect them to. They weren't wild about my multicolored henhouse, either."

"I could mention a few things of yours that I'm wild about."

"Dan, cut it out. Besides, you'll only make this worse. Maybe it's good for us to have some time apart. We'll be able to think about our situation without . . . well, you know."

His voice was low and sexy as he teased her. "Without what?"

"You know I can't think straight when we're . . . when you're . . ."

"Kissing you all over?" Dan supplied helpfully.

"That's enough."

"It's never been enough. How I love touching those sweet, secret—"

"Dan!"

"Places that make you quiver while you beg me to—"

The line clicked.

"And no matter how much you beg me to consider the cemetery fence, I know that my grandmother would definitely have wanted the library roof repaired," Dan finished in a businesslike tone.

"April, are you using the telephone, honey?"

"Yes, Mrs. Ordway, but I'll be through in a few minutes."

"Don't rush, honey. Sounds like long distance."

Dan spoke. "Yes, this is Dan Butler, Mrs. Ordway."

"Why, Dan, how nice to hear from you."

"Actually I was calling April."

"Well, of course you were. I'll get right off the phone and let you two young people chat."

April jumped in before she could hang up. "Just some board business, Mrs. Ordway. Nothing important."

"Board business on a Friday night? My, but you two are really dedicated."

"You don't know how much," Dan said fervently. "Good night, Mrs. Ordway."

"Good night, dear."

April was torn between laughter and fury. Laughter won out. "You are going to land us both in a pile of manure," she said when she could talk again.

"This is ridiculous. In Chicago we can be lovers and nobody cares. Now that you're in Booneville, I can't even talk to you on the telephone."

"That's the way it works."

"When are you going to spring your sculpture on Henry Goodpasture?"

"Next week. I'm setting up a combined meeting of the beautification committee and the board here at my house on Tuesday night. Would you like to be here?"

"You don't even have to ask, but under the circumstances I'd better stay away. I really don't want to influence this decision one way or the other, April. Right now my feelings for you are playing havoc with my better judgment."

"Good."

"Maybe not so good for the town. Booneville needs a cool head running this board."

"You've always been very good at that sort of thing."

"That was before I made love to you."

April savored his statement for a moment. "I wish you were here," she said gently.

"That makes two of us. Try to manufacture some reason that makes my presence in Booneville necessary, will you?"

"You might not approve of my methods."

Dan groaned. "Probably not. Just get this sculpture thing over with, okay? Once that's settled, one way or the other, we can concentrate on our own situation."

"Did it ever occur to you that the sculpture *is* part of our situation?"

Dan was silent on the other end of the line. "I was afraid of that," he said finally. "April, will you do me a favor?"

"What?"

"Wear that darn ring to bed tonight."

PUTTING ON the emerald-and-diamond ring each night became a sweet ritual for April. When she slipped it on her finger and turned out the light, she felt Dan's presence draw nearer. Her need for him was stronger, it seemed, while she wore the ring, but she welcomed the emotional pull toward the man who made her feel so alive.

On Tuesday night she finished her chores early so she could prepare for the evening ahead. She wore her forest-green dress and her glasses and even went so far as to pull her hair back into a bun. Earlier in the day she'd baked three pumpkin pies, Henry's favorite dessert, and dusted off the silver tea service that Bess Easley and her husband had given as a wedding present when April married Jimmy.

Positioning the sculpture in the living room had taken the better part of Monday. No matter where she put it, the sweeping modern design shouted its presence amid the comfortable but uninspired furniture April had inherited from her parents when they moved out. Years ago she'd begged her mother to take everything to their new home, but her mother understandably had wanted to start over and had saved April a large amount of money in the process.

But now, because she didn't yet have the pedestal Erica had promised, April longed for some sort of stand that would support the sculpture with a trace of style. At last she draped an end table with a white linen tablecloth and set the sculpture on that. It would have to do. Then, as a touch of drama, she placed a second tablecloth over the sculpture so she could have an unveiling.

Bill and Ida Mae Lowdermilk arrived first, and Bill insisted on peeking under the tablecloth.

"I can't tell what it is," he complained. "Can't we take this thing off?"

"I thought everyone should see it at once," April said, steering him away from the corner containing the sculpture. "Besides, you'll love it."

"I will?"

Ida Mae stuck her head in from the kitchen where she was brewing coffee. "You certainly will, darling."

"How do you know, Idie? You haven't seen it, either."

"I know, but I believe in April's choice. And Dan was in on this, too, don't forget."

"Not exactly," April said. "He's not really for or against having this type of sculpture on the square."

Bill glanced at her. "Diplomatic of him, isn't it?"

"He wants to give the rest of you a chance to decide without his opinion."

"He doesn't like it," Bill concluded.

"No, I didn't say that. He—" The doorbell saved April from further explanation, and she went to welcome the next arrivals.

Within ten minutes her living room was filled with people. Gerald Sloan and M.G. Tucker, the two bachelors, had elected to come together; despite their differences in philosophy, they maintained a cordial relationship. Bess Easley had asked if her husband, George, could come along because she hated to drive alone at night, so George was the only member of the group who wasn't actively involved in the project. Mabel and Henry Goodpasture arrived late and argued all the way in the door.

With Ida Mae's help April settled everyone with pie and coffee before mentioning the tablecloth-draped sculpture in the corner. She noticed everyone glancing uneasily toward the ghostly object, but the conversation turned to other subjects, including the Booneville High Bulldogs' chances to take a state title in football and how much the rain had affected the fall harvest.

When the plates were clean and everyone but Henry had declined seconds, April took charge of the gathering. She liked the idea of doing so while Henry still had his mouth full of pumpkin pie.

"As you all know, I spent a few days in Chicago last week looking for a sculptor to design something for the square," she began.

"I hear Chicago was pretty cold last week," George Easley volunteered.

"I guess so." April remembered it as being quite warm indeed, but that had little to do with the weather. She hoped she wasn't blushing. "As all of you also know, I didn't have a great deal of money to offer someone. Nevertheless, I've found a talented sculptor who is willing to work for little more than the materials involved. That's a fantastic deal, and we're lucky to find someone so dedicated to art."

"What's under the sheet?" Henry asked, finally voicing the question that had hung in the air all evening. "Did he make us a miniature or something?"

"In a way, yes." April started to correct Henry's statement and announce that the sculptor was a woman, but then she quickly reconsidered. The gender of the artist shouldn't matter, but to someone like Henry, and maybe even Gerald Sloan, it might. She'd keep that secret for a while.

"He must be a fast worker," M.G. commented.

"The sculpture I'm about to show you wasn't created for us," April said. "I saw it in a gallery window and bought it. Then I asked for the name of the artist and we made our deal—contingent, of course, on the approval of this group."

"But Dan's not here," Gerald Sloan said. "Are we to assume he approves of this choice?"

April took a deep breath. "Dan wanted to withhold his judgment until each of you had a chance to form an opinion."

"I thought he was supervising all of this," Henry said.

April glanced at the banker. How she would love to take the rest of the pie from the kitchen and smash it into his face. "That's true, but when Dan realized that I had a definite idea of what I wanted, he stepped back and allowed me to work somewhat independently. I take full responsibility for this decision."

"Well, let's see this thing in the corner, then," Henry said with a sigh.

April crossed to the sculpture and paused. Her palms were damp with anxiety. "The work for the square won't be exactly like this, but the style will be similar. Just imagine this one about fifteen feet tall instead of two, and you'll get a mental picture of what it will look like." She grasped the tablecloth and whipped it away from the sculpture.

The gasp of surprise came almost in unison. April had expected that. The sculpture was breathtaking. But as she turned toward her seated guests, she gulped. The look on everyone's face, including that of her dear friend Ida Mae, was of unmitigated horror.

## 10

HENRY WAS THE FIRST to bellow his response. "A fifteen-foot dead tree stump? Not with my money!"

"But it's not your money," April countered.

"I beg to differ, young lady. The money belongs to all of us, all the people of Booneville. And I'd like to emphasize—" he paused to point a finger at her "—it's not *your* money."

Mabel Goodpasture stood up. Her initial shocked expression had been replaced with one of defiance as she peered down at her husband over the jut of her ample bosom. "I love this piece of art," she announced. "I think something like this will look lovely on the square."

April closed her eyes. She wanted support, not an extension of a family feud.

"You can't be serious, Mabel," Henry retorted. "Bill can take his tractor down by the river and drag something like this back here for free."

"April has been to Europe, Henry, which you certainly have not. She has a great deal more cultural experience than some people I could mention."

April groaned. "Please, Mabel, I—"

Bess Easley, the peacemaker, intervened. "April, does this piece of sculpture have a name or something? I think it looks a bit like a figure, there, with the hands, no . . . maybe the whole thing is one hand, sort of—"

"Sort of like our kids make with clay in nursery school," Bill Lowdermilk finished, ignoring Ida Mae's urgent tug on his sleeve.

"The sculpture is called *Impulse*, Bess," April said.

Gerald Sloan laughed. "And an unfortunate impulse it was, too. Of course, if a guy can get good money for this kind of junk, I suppose he's a genius, after all."

"That's for sure," Henry added with a chuckle. "Maybe I should start hacking out things like this and give up banking. Must not take more than ten minutes to do one, wouldn't you say, M.G.?"

"Oh, I wouldn't be that hasty about the amount of work that went into this, Henry. There's a certain elegance there. I'd like a little while to think this one over before we decide anything."

Ida Mae applauded. "What an excellent idea. Let's all go home and think before we make any final decisions." She jabbed Bill in the ribs when he looked as if he might object.

"A few days won't change my mind," Henry said, crossing his arms and leaning back in his chair. "How about you, Gerry?"

"I doubt it. This is a far cry from Grant on his horse, which was a darn good suggestion, in my opinion."

"I'm beginning to like it more and more," Bess said, cocking her head to one side. "It does look like impulse, now that I study the shape more. Don't you think so, George?"

Her husband shook his head. "I'm staying out of this."

Mabel walked over and placed her hand on the sculpture as if to give it her blessing. "I'm in favor of April's choice, and that's that."

"And I'm not, and that's that," Henry said.

"And I say let's all sleep on it," Ida Mae said, standing.

"If we're going to do that, I want Dan in on the next meeting," Henry announced. "He can't hide up there in Chicago while we battle everything out down here. I'm calling him tonight. Maybe he can be here this weekend."

April stared at Henry. Dan's wish would come true. He'd have a valid reason to visit Booneville. But when he heard what it was, he might not be so eager for the trip.

Dan's late-night phone call to April confirmed her fear that he wasn't happy with this turn of events.

"I thought after tonight it would be settled," he said. "Who supported you?"

"You expected me to be shot down immediately, didn't you?"

"Frankly, yes."

"Thanks a lot."

"April, this sculpture is folly. You may convince a few of your loyal followers that it isn't, but the townspeople will not like this project, believe me."

"So come down and vote against me. You have Henry and Gerry on your side right off the bat. Bill may vote against the sculpture, too, so your negative vote would finish me off."

"That may be exactly what happens. Can you handle that?"

"Sure."

"And then what about us?"

"I don't know."

"I do, and you were right about this sculpture being part of our situation. You're going to blame me if this project doesn't go through."

"You could make a big difference if you wanted to."

"Listen, I can't imagine this thing on the town square. What's more, I'm afraid erecting it with my grandmother's money will set the town against the whole concept of her legacy."

"No, that won't happen."

"It might. April, you can't force your concept of art down the townspeople's throats and expect them to swallow it."

"I wouldn't force, I would educate. It could be done. You should have seen Bess Easley. At first she reacted against the sculpture, but gradually she began to appreciate it, and before she left, she really liked the concept."

"Bess admires you. You won't get that kind of cooperation from everyone else in town."

"And certainly not from you."

"April, I— Oh, hell. I'll see you Saturday."

"Are we meeting in the bank again?"

"No. That was a bad idea last time, and whether you think I side with Henry or not, I don't want him to have an unfair advantage. He does in that building."

"I'm glad you realize that."

"We'll meet at Jesse's café."

"That's nice and private. Only half the county comes in for a cup of coffee every morning."

"Jesse's agreed to close down for a half hour, from ten to ten-thirty. It shouldn't take much longer than that."

"Not if everyone's mind is made up."

Dan sighed. "By the way, are you still wearing the ring to bed?"

"I'm not telling."

"I don't know why I asked. I don't believe in the damn thing anyway. Good night, April."

"Good night, Dan." April replaced the receiver in its cradle and gazed into the green depths of the ring on her finger. Dan might believe in its powers if he knew that he'd become her obsession, just as he'd said he wanted to be.

No matter what inauspicious circumstances were bringing him to her, she wanted desperately to see him again. Even his rejection of the sculpture and the harsh words they'd exchanged couldn't blunt the razor-sharp edge of her passion. Whether lust or love ruled her heart she wasn't sure. She only knew she had to have him back in her arms once more, no matter what the cost.

JESSE HARDCASTLE WAS one of the few women in Booneville besides April who ran her own business. Unlike April, however, she declined to take part in community projects, claiming that she and her café were the Switzerland of their little world, an oasis of neutrality in a hotbed of strong allegiances.

April respected her stand and realized the wisdom of it, considering that Jesse would find herself defending her chosen opinions every day of the week and might very well lose customers who didn't agree with her. For April, controversy wasn't nearly as dangerous because her customers seldom lingered to converse over a cup of coffee the way Jesse's did.

Jesse's Café, on the northwest corner of the square and catty-corner from Henry's bank, was the obvious location to hold the board meeting, provided Jesse agreed to hang her Closed sign on the door for the duration of the meeting. When April drove past the café just before ten on Saturday morning, the sign was already in place.

April could see her breath in the bitterly cold morning air as she parked the truck on the square and walked toward the café. During her round of chores before daylight, April could have sworn that a few snowflakes touched her face, and the leaden clouds that now covered the sun indicated that winter would come early to Booneville this year.

The café's windows gleamed a bright welcome. Anxious to get out of the cold but even more anxious to see Dan, April hurried toward the door. Then she deliberately slowed her step. The other members of the board must not suspect that she and Dan had become lovers while she was in Chicago. Her entrance had to be sedate, her greeting to Dan nonchalant. Only he would attribute significance to her choice of contacts over glasses this morning.

Through the clear panes of the door April noticed that the men had pushed two tables together to provide enough room, and Jesse was plying everyone with steaming mugs of coffee and her morning's delivery of Danish. Dan was facing the door and laughing about something.

He hadn't seen her, and for a moment April stood outside the café and savored the sight of him. Like everyone else at the table, he'd dressed for the cold. April was pleased that he still owned a plaid flannel shirt and could slip back into the country atmosphere of Jesse's Café without seeming out of place. In that instant she knew she wanted Dan to come home again for good. Yet he'd told her how he felt about farming. He'd no more be satisfied with chickens than Jimmy had been.

With a sigh April opened the door. The tiny silver bell attached to the inside jingled, and the men stopped talking and turned toward her. "Hi," she said with what she hoped was a jaunty smile. "Any Danish left for me?"

"You bet," Bill said, starting to rise. The others followed suit.

"Nobody gets up, remember?"

"Right," they all chorused and sat down again.

The only empty seat was next to Dan. April took off her old quilted jacket and draped it over the chair. She'd had to go for warmth instead of looks today, including jeans instead of a dress and a yellow cable-knit sweater. While sitting down she allowed herself the merest glance at Dan's face. April looked away quickly. Could everyone else see the emotion shining in those blue eyes? If so, the lovers' secret would be out in seconds.

Jesse bustled in from the kitchen with another mug and a fresh pot of coffee. "Here you are, April," she said, placing the mug on the table and filling it from the pot in her hand. "And I heard that remark about the Danish. You know I wouldn't let these characters devour everything. I saved one of your favorites, strawberry. Want me to heat it up with a pat of butter?"

"Jesse, you know my weaknesses." Instantly April regretted her choice of words as Dan nudged her under the table with his knee.

"She certainly knows mine," M.G. said as he bit into his pastry. "I hate to tell you, Henry, but this beats all heck out of meeting in the bank. You didn't offer us so much as a toothpick and water."

"Pay me for the service and I will, M.G. Jesse's not donating the refreshments, last I heard."

"Not on your life," Jesse said, returning with April's warm Danish. "I should charge you double this morning. Cold Saturday like this, all the farmers come in for miles around, and I'm losing their business."

"We'll be gone by ten-thirty. I promise, Jesse," Dan said. "And we appreciate your letting us have the place at all."

Jesse grinned. "I'll probably do a landslide business when you clear out. Everyone will want to know what you talked about."

"And you're free to tell them," Dan said, "as long as you get the facts straight. Everyone agreed?"

The rest of the board members nodded.

"We don't want to have secrets," M.G. commented. "Just a little peace and quiet while we work things out."

"Then I'll sit right over here and listen." Jesse chose a table nearby and sat down expectantly.

"And I guess we'd better get started," Dan said. "I understand all of you have seen April's sculpture."

"Have we ever!" Henry exclaimed. "Did she even show it to you while she was in Chicago? I can't believe you let her get by with that monstrosity."

M.G. cleared his throat. "Let's eliminate name-calling from this discussion, shall we? To many people the sculpture is a fine work of art, not a monstrosity."

"Oh, Lord." Henry slapped his forehead. "M.G.'s turning cultural on us."

"We'll proceed with this in an orderly fashion," Dan said firmly. "But first let me straighten one thing out, Henry. I saw my role as April's advisor, not some sort of tyrant who would dictate her choice."

April thrilled to his tone of command and his defense of her actions. Maybe, just maybe, he'd come through for her after all.

Gerald Sloan put down his coffee mug. "And what, as her advisor, did you say when you saw the sculpture and learned that she intended something very much like it to rise on yon town square?" The lawyer gestured toward the door of the café.

"I said I thought it was inappropriate."

April cringed. Dan's knee pressed hard against hers under the table, and she knew he was trying to tell her he cared, despite what he felt obliged to say.

"That's my boy," Henry said with an approving nod.

"However, she disagreed with me. Had we voted between the two of us, we would have had a tie, so I decided perhaps she should present the idea to the rest of you.

Frankly I expected all four of you to reject it. That would have settled the matter."

M.G. shifted in his chair and adjusted his wire-rimmed glasses. "I'd like to say something. When April first pulled the tablecloth off the statue, or sculpture, or whatever, I reacted like everyone else in the room. But the thing grows on you, maybe because you can look at it a million times and see something different each time. A soldier on a horse is a soldier on a horse, period. But this . . . we might never get tired of it."

April smiled at him. "Thanks, M.G."

"And another thing. I wouldn't be surprised if Irene would have loved it."

"You're right, M.G.," April said quickly. "In fact—"

Gerald Sloan cut her off. "That's speculation."

"I'm glad I have a lawyer on my side," Henry said with a chuckle.

Dan turned to Bill. "You've been pretty quiet through all of this. What's your opinion?"

"Well, it keeps changing, Dan, according to whether I feel like being in the doghouse with my wife or not."

Everyone laughed, including April. Ida Mae was loyal to the end, and she was insisting that her husband be, too.

"But seriously," Bill continued, "I was put on this board, not my wife, and I will make an independent decision." With that remark he looked directly at Henry. "The strange thing is that every day that goes by, I become more intrigued with April's idea. That sculpture on the square would show people around here that Booneville is a progressive town. I like that."

"We'll show them that we're idiots who will spend thousands of dollars on nothing," Henry said with a sneer.

Emboldened by M.G. and Bill's support, April spoke. "Thousands of dollars on a thing of beauty, Henry. And here's something you should appreciate. We'll be getting a real bargain. The amount of money we're offering is only enough to cover materials for a large sculpture like that, which would be true of a soldier on a horse, too, I suppose. Anyway, the artist has agreed to do the work and make nothing on it."

"I can understand that," Henry said, obviously unswayed by her argument. "There's not much work to be done in the first place. Give me the money, and I'll make you something just as good. Maybe better."

April clenched her coffee cup. "Henry Goodpasture, your ego is—"

"April." Dan's hand covered hers.

His gentle touch silenced her as nothing else could have. Instead of dwelling on Henry's obnoxious behavior, she was busy dealing with the warmth of Dan's fingers and the memory of how expertly he had stroked her naked body.

He left his hand on hers for just a moment, not enough to rouse the suspicions of the people around the table. "I would call for a vote at this point, but I'm reluctant to do that. We could have a tie, and if we can't break it, we'll lose the entire legacy. I'd rather not risk voting now when we might end up with an unbreakable stalemate."

April looked at him. A tie. If M.G., Bill and she were on one side, that meant Dan considered himself on the other side. She could only guess how much it was costing him emotionally to deny her what she wanted. Despite her disappointment that he couldn't imagine the sculpture on the square, she grudgingly admired him for sticking with his beliefs and risking her displeasure.

"I think we could do with some input, some public opinion, before we vote," M.G. suggested.

Dan shook his head. "The townspeople couldn't have much of an opinion until they see April's sculpture and have some idea of what we're talking about. She can't have a parade through her living room. She'd never get any work done."

Jesse stood up. "I've been trying to figure this out. How could something you're considering for the square fit in April's living room?"

"It's a smaller sculpture, Jesse," April explained, "and it will only give people an idea of what to expect for the larger one. As to turning my living room into an art gallery, I don't mind if that's what it takes."

"Why not put your sculpture in the café?" Jesse suggested. "You'll have the exposure, and I'll attract more customers."

April smiled. "You're a true businesswoman, Jesse."

"I think that's a great idea," M.G. said. "If April doesn't mind. After all, the sculpture is her property."

"I don't mind. I know Jesse will take good care of it."

Dan glanced around the table again. "Does this suit everyone?"

Henry frowned. "Well, we can't have a vote now, that's for sure, or we'll put all the projects on the line. But I say we leave the statue in here for a week and then vote. We'll know what public opinion is by then, although I can already tell you nobody will want that thing."

"I'd prefer two weeks," April said, thinking quickly. "Next Saturday night I'd like to invite the sculptor down to give a talk somewhere, maybe in the 4-H building, about the work. Then we can vote the following weekend."

"That might be interesting," M.G. said.

Henry snorted. "We're just dragging out the inevitable, but I can see some of you want to turn this into a circus. I can't save you from your foolishness, so go ahead and take your two weeks."

"All agreed?" Dan asked once more and received a chorus of affirmative answers. "Then let's leave so that Jesse can open for the thriving business she expects once we're gone."

As they stood and bundled up in their heavy coats and all the men except Dan pulled on caps, April wondered how to speak to Dan alone. Surely he wouldn't drive back to Chicago today without stopping by her house on the way out of town. Last time he'd done that, she'd sent him away before their emotions could overwhelm them. This time she wouldn't be so prudish—if he arrived on her doorstep at all.

"Bet I surprised you, huh?" Bill took her elbow as the crowd headed for the door.

"A pleasant surprise," April answered, smiling up at him. "Thanks, Bill. Idie should bake you a whole batch of frosted brownies for that."

"She's tried to bribe me with food all week, but I really did make up my own mind."

"I know. That's what makes it more special. You really believe in what I'm trying to do."

"And so do I," M.G. added, coming to her other side. "We'll get support for the idea. Have faith, April."

"With you two on my side, how can I help it? I wish Irene could be here to be a part of all this."

M.G. looked wistful. "Yeah. But of course if she were still alive, you'd be having bake sales forever just to pay for the sculpture. She wasn't about to tell us she was rich."

"No, and I've decided that was very wise of her," April said. She watched Dan go through the door ahead of them, and she began to panic. What if he left, certain that she was angry enough not to want to see him? She thought quickly. "If you'll excuse me, I'm going to ask Dan to contact the sculptor when he gets back to Chicago. That'll save me a long-distance call."

"Good idea," M.G. said. "And I'm glad you're asking him down. I'd like to meet the guy who created *Impulse*."

April hurried forward and reached Dan just as he was starting the Honda's engine. He rolled down the window at her approach.

"About the sculptor," she said in a voice loud enough for the departing board members to hear. "Could you make the contact for me so I don't have to call long distance?"

Dan lifted an eyebrow questioningly, but his answer was casual. "Sure."

April rested her hands on the open window of the car and lowered her voice. "Driving back today?"

He gazed at her intently. "Why, are you anxious for me to call Erica this afternoon?"

"Not necessarily. I was wondering if you'd care to drop by on your way out of town. It seems a shame to travel all the way down and all the way back without picking up a dozen fresh eggs. They wouldn't spoil between here and Chicago. You could have them with your Sunday breakfast."

"I seldom eat breakfast when I'm alone."

"What a shame."

"That I seldom eat breakfast?"

"No, that you're planning to be alone tomorrow morning." The others were gone by now, and she leaned a little closer. "When was the last time you watched a sunrise over a multicolored henhouse?"

He looked at her in disbelief. "I just shot you down in there."

"I know."

"Yet you're issuing me an invitation."

"That's right. Care to accept?"

His hands tightened on the steering wheel, and passion flared in his eyes. "I may be slow, but I'm no fool."

"Then I'll meet you there."

"Just a minute. What about parking the car outside? Red is a very visible color."

"I think there's room in the old barn."

He gazed at her for a long moment. "If we're going to do this, there's something you should know."

"What's that?"

"I . . . the games are over for me, April."

"What do you mean?"

"I'm in love with you."

# 11

APRIL CLUTCHED THE CAR DOOR for support. "Why are you telling me that here? Why now?"

"In case you want to change your mind about that invitation. In case you thought going to bed with me will be a carefree experience with no strings attached. It won't."

"Dan, you may be sure about your feelings, but I'm not. What if I hurt you again? What if—"

"It's too late, April. If I lose you again, it will be agony, but I don't intend to lose you. I made up my mind when you walked into the café this morning that whatever happens with the sculpture isn't going to keep us apart. Temporarily it might be a problem, like this morning. I thought you'd be angry about all this and wouldn't want much to do with me for a while."

She averted her gaze. Making this overture to him, after what had taken place in the café, revealed a lot about her state of mind concerning Dan. She glanced at his strong hands as they rested on the steering wheel. No matter what had happened, she wanted him to touch her again, love her again. "Maybe I'm not strong enough to stand on principle right now." She looked into his eyes. "Or maybe it's that crazy emerald."

"You've been wearing it."

"At night. Yes."

"I may become a believer yet." Slowly he stroked the length of her bare ring finger and his voice grew husky.

"Why don't you drive home, and I'll be there in a little while."

"Henry and Mabel's again?"

He shook his head. "M.G. He wants to see me about something."

April turned her hand over and squeezed his. "Don't stay long."

"No way. And you drive safely."

"I will." April gave his hand one more squeeze and hurried away to her truck. He loved her. Even though she'd sensed it before, hearing it confirmed really shook her. He had the courage to say the words out loud while she'd avoided even thinking them.

Twice in her life she'd spoken words of love to a man. The first time, with Dan, had been the product of a young girl's fantasy, a dream destined to be shattered. The second time, with Jimmy, had been infatuation born partially of her disillusionment with Dan. April wondered if the unspoken emotion that gripped her now might be the real thing. She wanted to be sure before blurting out words that contained such power.

The inside of the truck was cold, and she turned on the heater. Raindrops splashed against the windshield as she drove down the two-lane country road away from town. Shaky with excitement, she began making plans for their next few hours together. The weather should keep away visitors and customers. With a little luck, they could have the night to themselves. All to themselves.

By the time she heard a car in the lane leading to the house, she'd set the scene. He'd admitted loving her, but she wanted more. She wanted him to love this haven in the country, too. He'd grown up in a house like this; the sweet memories were there for her to draw from, and instinct told her Dan wasn't yet a confirmed city boy.

It was raining in earnest now, and she pulled on boots and a yellow slicker and hat before hurrying out to open the barn door for him. Long ago the barn had been used for a few cows and one horse, but the large livestock had been sold years ago, and the barn was only for storage now. Someday April planned to paint it different colors, too.

When he saw her, he started to get out of the car, but she waved him back in and sloshed through the rain to the barn. He drove behind her but got out again when she struggled with the heavy sliding door.

"I can do it. You'll be soaked," she protested as he came to her side.

He grinned at her and reached for the heavy door. "I guess that means I'll have to take my clothes off and get dry."

"I hadn't thought of that."

"Obviously. You wore a raincoat."

April laughed as together they pushed the door aside. She stepped into the dim interior of the barn while Dan returned to the car and drove it inside. The Honda fit into the center aisle of the barn with ease.

"I saw your Eggs Sold Out sign by the road," Dan said as he climbed out of the car and walked back to her. "Does that mean I don't get my dozen?"

"Do you believe everything you read?"

"Ah, subterfuge." He smiled and touched her damp cheek with the palm of his hand. "I was wondering if any of your customers would be out in this weather."

"No point in taking chances." She turned her head and kissed his palm.

"No," he said with a smile. He framed her face with both hands and tilted it up to his. "You look like an ad for Morton Salt. I especially like the rain hat."

"You could have done with a hat," she replied, reaching up to wipe a drop of water from his cheek. "Your hair is dripping."

"I don't care. It's been a long time since I've gotten soaked in a rainstorm." He studied her lovingly. "You know, I like the smell of this old barn. It reminds me of a certain rainy afternoon a long time ago, about this time of year. Two kids got trapped during a downpour and scurried in here to keep dry. Then they huddled together to keep warm. And then . . . Do you remember?"

"I'm surprised that you do," April said in a voice as soft as the rain on the old barn roof. "I thought only girls remembered a first kiss."

He slipped his hand under her damp hair and caressed the nape of her neck. "I have a memory like an elephant when it comes to you." Gently he urged her closer and took off her hat with his other hand. "For old time's sake," he murmured, tilting her head back and brushing her lips with his.

At her small, nearly inaudible moan he lifted his head and looked into her eyes. The raw hunger reflected there took his breath away. Dropping her hat to the barn floor he hauled her, heavy slicker and all, into his arms and kissed her hard. She was ready for him, her lips yielding and warm, her mouth open to receive the thrust of his tongue.

The taste of her inflamed him after long nights without her. Immediately he felt the primitive beat of arousal pounding through his veins, and he fought with the metal clasps of her rain-slick coat.

At last the coat was open, her softness accessible. He held her tightly and rubbed the lower half of his body against her in a vain attempt to ease the pulsing heat she evoked with only a kiss. He had to love her, had to bury himself deep within her. But not here. They didn't have to settle for a blanket on a cold barn floor. Not now.

He left the invitation of her lips reluctantly and refastened her coat. "Come on," he said, steering her toward the door. "This old barn was great for a couple of kids, but we're not kids anymore. I'm taking you to bed."

They raced through the rain holding hands and dodging puddles. On the front porch April took off her boots and rain gear and advised Dan to kick off his muddy shoes.

"We can dry the rest inside," she said, tossing her coat on the porch swing and opening the front door.

Dan followed her into the warmth of the living room and felt as if he'd come home. A fire in the hearth dispelled all the gloom of the rainy day and turned the house into a cozy refuge. He remembered the furniture from their dating days. Many times he'd sat on the couch's floral-print cushions talking to her mother and father while April got ready for a movie or a school dance.

The last time he'd sat there, he'd been wearing a tux and feeling like a big man on campus after nearly two years at Blackburn. And then April had come down the stairs, looking like a vision in a pale yellow chiffon dress. His April . . . Yet in the end she hadn't been his, had she? This house was where she'd lived with someone else, where they'd— He glanced toward the downstairs bedroom.

"Dan?"

He turned to see her standing in her sock feet with her hand out.

"I asked if I could take your jacket, but you didn't seem to hear me."

He unzipped the damp jacket and peeled it away from his flannel shirt. "Sorry."

"Dan—"

"I guess reminiscing comes easily in Booneville. This room . . . I remember the last time we . . . Oh, April!" He swept her into his arms and buried his face against her neck. "I'm going to love you until you forget there ever was another man."

April became completely still in his arms. She'd seen him glance toward the bedroom and had assumed he was imagining their lovemaking there. Until this moment she'd forgotten about Jimmy, and that she'd shared that room with him until their divorce. After two years without him she'd come to think of the master bedroom downstairs as hers, not theirs. But for Dan that passage of time had little meaning, especially when he had just relived a last date that had taken place eight years ago.

"Dan." She eased away from him and cradled his face in her hands. "Forgive me. I didn't think. We can go upstairs."

"No." He drew her back against him. "I want to banish him from there. I want to replace his memory with mine."

Tears misted her eyes. "I never really loved him."

His tone was gentle. "You never really loved me, either, did you?"

"Not enough, Dan. Not nearly enough. But I was just a silly girl."

"Silly, maybe, and beautiful and headstrong." He took a deep breath. "I thought I loved you then, but it was nothing like this."

"No." Eyes brimming, she shook her head. "Not for me, either." She took his hand. "And I'm going to make love to you until you forget everything but this moment."

He realized later that she kept her promise. When they stepped inside the bedroom, he stood in the doorway and watched her undress. With her deliberate, seductive motions the past faded from his mind, and the future lost its power to threaten. Her body gleamed in the soft light from the casement window. Piece by piece her clothing fell to the floor.

When the last of it was gone, she remained there for a moment and let him look at her. Shadows from the raindrops coursing down the windowpane traced liquid patterns on her creamy skin. He became mesmerized by the rain shadows as he followed their sliding path down the slope of her breasts to the nippled peaks and beyond, to the curve of her ribs, her smooth belly and the dark curls below.

The chill air seeping in around the window frame smelled of the rain, damp and fertile. The room was cool, yet she didn't seem to feel the cold. Slowly she walked across the hardwood floor to her nightstand and picked up an object lying there. Only when she placed it on her finger did he realize what it was.

Then, wearing only the ring, she came to him. The ancient creak of the wood mingled with the patter of the rain were the only sounds in the room, sounds that would never be the same for him again. He closed his eyes as she began unbuttoning his flannel shirt.

She took her time. When he murmured his impatience and tried to help her with the various fastenings, she moved his hand away with a tiny shake of her head.

"You're in the country now," she said, her voice rhythmic and musical, blending with the rain. "Life moves slower here."

She tortured him with her butterfly touch while she took away the last of his clothing and revealed the full extent of his arousal. With superhuman effort he restrained his impulse to crush her in his arms and take what he needed. Instead, he followed her lead as they stretched out on the brass bedstead.

His senses had never been more alive to his surroundings . . . the floral scent of the sheets, the sound of the bedsprings under them, the moist press of April's lips on his eyelids, his cheeks, his chin and at last his mouth. Her fragrant hair swung down against his cheek, and her nipples brushed lazily against his chest as she ran her tongue over the sensitive inside of his mouth. He thought he would come apart.

Yet as her kisses moved down the column of his neck, he knew she wasn't through with him. His breathing accelerated with the downward progress she made, and when she reached her destination, he cried out in response to the sweet agony of her tongue and lips teasing his throbbing flesh. When he thought he could stand no more, he wove his fingers through her hair.

"Enough," he said, panting. "April, I can't—"

She retraced her path and kissed him on the mouth. "You're doing fine," she whispered, moving over him, "just fine."

"Wait. I haven't done anything about—"

"It was my responsibility this time. Don't worry." Gently she lowered herself, taking him gradually deep inside as she watched the pleasure sweep over him. His pleasure was hers; his joy filled her with happiness. April knew the truth at last. "I love you, too," she murmured.

He gripped her shoulders, and twin flames sprang to life in his eyes. His words came out in a hoarse croak. "What did you say?"

"I love you, Dan."

"You're sure?"

"Yes."

"Then nothing else matters."

"Nothing but this." She rotated her hips in a slow circle and then reversed the motion.

Dan moaned and looked at her through glazed eyes. "You're driving me crazy."

"That's the idea." She began to rock back and forth, and he picked up her rhythm, pressing upward to increase the friction that was fanning the blaze of their desire into a bonfire of passion.

April writhed against him, and the bedsprings sang with their movements. She had never given so much, nor received so much in return. With every motion of her body she told him of her love, and he answered in kind. The sound of the rain accompanied the soft sounds that grew to exultant cries of release as the lovers shuddered together in a drenching climax.

For a long while Dan lay still, holding her tight and listening to the rain. Finally he reached for her hand as it lay limply on the pillow beside his head. The ring that had felt cold each time he took it from his dresser drawer was warm now from her heat, her unbridled response to him. He wanted to ask her to keep it forever, but he hesitated. She'd admitted her love. Maybe that was enough for now.

She lifted her head, and her brown eyes were warm as she gazed down at him. "Now do you believe?"

"At this very moment you could convince me of anything."

Immediately April thought of the sculpture. Perhaps she could ask him now to support her wishes, and he would agree. Yet she wouldn't do that. Trading on what they had just shared to get her way would diminish their newfound love for each other.

She smiled. "How about if I try to convince you that evening chores on a chicken farm are exciting and fun?" she asked instead.

"Do we have to leave this bed to find out?"

"I'm afraid so."

"Somehow I knew that. Can we come back afterward?"

"I was counting on it."

He ruffled her hair. "Then let's get going. But don't think you can turn me into a farm boy by promising fringe benefits."

"I won't." Yet she wondered if that was exactly what she was hoping to do. She'd grown up watching her mother and father work together on the farm. It wasn't a bad life. She sympathized with Dan's feelings, especially considering that his father had been killed in a farming accident, but she wished he would open his mind a little more.

Dan was cheerful enough as they tended to the chickens and settled them for the night. Chores were lighter at this time of year, and for that April was glad. How would Dan react to the more arduous seasons of spring and summer?

When they returned to the house, Dan stoked the fire, and April heated up the homemade vegetable soup she'd planned for dinner. She'd made bread earlier in the week, and on a trip to Springfield she'd picked up some of the wine Dan had served her in Chicago. The meal would be simple but good, just as she wanted him to perceive her life-style here. How could he possibly resist it?

They ate perched on pillows by the fire. As she served Dan seconds of soup and hot slices of buttered bread, she casually mentioned that she'd made both herself.

"I'm getting the picture, April," Dan said with a wry smile. "My favorite wine, home-cooked food, a cozy fire in a wonderful old farmhouse on a rainy night. I'd be a fool not to prefer all of this to my place in Chicago. And I do. But the price you have to pay is too high."

"Are you talking about your father?"

"Some. But more than that is the insecurity. A really bad heat wave could kill half your chickens. Cold is dangerous, too. Lack of rain or too much at the wrong times could ruin your produce for that season. You're totally dependent upon Mother Nature, and she's a fickle gal."

"Maybe I'm dependent on the weather, like you say, but I'm not tied to a boss. I'm my own boss. I like that."

"I would, too, but not under these circumstances."

She gave him a long look. "I don't want to leave this farm, Dan."

"I know you don't."

"It's a long commute from Chicago."

"I know that, too."

"Then?"

"I'm working on it." He glanced at her. "Sounds as if you've considered extending this relationship."

"Maybe."

"Especially if I'm willing to take up farming?"

"Dan, is it really out of the question?"

"Yes."

She sighed in disappointment and frustration.

"Hey." He lifted her chin with one finger. "Don't give up on us just because I want to hitch my wagon to a star instead of a plow. Give me some time to find a solution."

April smiled uncertainly. "Okay."

"And I'm going to get myself another bowl of that fantastic soup."

She laughed. "I'll have to roll you out of here."

"Just so I can still fit through the bedroom door tonight." He winked and left for the kitchen.

"By the way," April asked when he returned, "can you tell me anything about what M.G. wanted, or was your conversation confidential?"

"I can tell you, and only you, because I think you should know, for a couple of reasons. He tried to convince me to approve the sculpture and break the inevitable tie."

"My goodness, he must be more dedicated to the idea than I thought."

"Maybe, but he's dedicated to the memory of my grandmother even more. They were lovers."

"*What?*"

"I know. I couldn't believe it, either, but then, she kept the secret of her fortune from all of us, so why not this?"

"The money was one thing, but I've never known a love affair to go unnoticed in Booneville. Too many eyes are watching, too many ears listening." April stared into the fire. "But I'm glad for them."

"You should also be glad for yourself. M.G. thought over this sculpture business and decided my grandmother would have wanted what you've proposed, so he'll be your staunch supporter forever. That's one reason I thought you should know about our conversation."

"But he didn't convince you?"

Dan shook his head. "He's operating from emotion. I'm trying to use logic." He looked at the sculpture sitting on its tablecloth-draped stand in the corner of the living room. "Logically that sort of sculpture doesn't fit on the square."

April started to argue that art wasn't ruled by logic, but she thought better of it. They'd been through this enough times, and Dan didn't seem likely to change his mind. "You said there were two reasons you needed to tell me about M.G."

"There are. At one point I asked him why he and my grandmother didn't make their situation official and get married."

"Good question. They were both free to do that, and the whole town would have given them its blessing."

"Well, M.G. wanted to marry her, and not because he knew anything about the money, either. He was in the dark like everyone else in town."

"I'm amazed. Irene was something else."

"She could keep her secrets when she wanted to. But she was painfully honest with M.G. when it came to her feelings for him. She said that he'd never replace my grandfather in her heart. There had been only one great passion in her life, a union that had been symbolized by an emerald-and-diamond heirloom ring."

April started and instinctively touched the emerald stone on her finger.

He noticed her gesture. "That's right, April. It's powerful medicine. Once it casts a spell, the two people involved will never be completely free of each other. I thought you should be warned."

She gazed into the blue depths of his eyes and remembered all the nights she'd worn the ring and longed to have his arms around her. The ring had worked its magic, and she was irrevocably in love with the man who'd given it to her. "To borrow a phrase from this morning—it's too late."

DAN LEFT SUNDAY AFTERNOON, and after her chores on Monday morning April took the sculpture to Jesse's Café. By the time she got home again, her telephone was already ringing, and the stream of calls kept coming for the next two days. No one's reaction was neutral; people either loved the sculpture or hated it. By Wednesday afternoon, when the Beautify Booneville committee met in the library, the entire town was choosing sides.

"I've told Henry he'd better vote for that sculpture or else," Mabel announced to the women gathered in the reading section of the library.

Bess looked at Mabel with curiosity. "Or else what?"

"He knows," Mabel said, and folded her arms.

April frowned as she guessed Mabel's possible form of coercion. "I would hate to think this issue was entering into yours and Henry's, ah, private life, Mabel."

"Can you tell me a faster way to make a man come around to your way of thinking? It's a time-honored method used by women."

Bess gasped. "Mabel, do you mean that you won't allow Henry to exercise his husbandly rights?"

"If you're asking if he's getting any exercise in the bedroom, the answer is no, not until he approves the sculpture."

"But, Mabel," Bess protested, her eyes wide, "what if he *never* votes for the sculpture?"

Mabel pursed her lips. "I don't think that will happen, Bess. Henry's a normal man, and you know how men are about that matter."

Ida Mae could contain herself no longer and began to laugh. "I can't believe this is happening," she chortled. "Sexual blackmail in Booneville."

"Well, what would you do, Idie, if your Bill hadn't already decided in favor of the sculpture?"

Ida Mae laughed harder. "My protests usually center around food," she admitted with a grin. "I can do without that easier."

"I don't think there should be any blackmail, sexual or otherwise," April said. "Really, Mabel, I wish you wouldn't resort to—" She bit the inside of her cheek to keep from laughing along with Ida Mae.

"It's the only thing that will work," Mabel said matter-of-factly. "He's the most pigheaded man in the world, and I have to deal with him as best I can. Now don't you ladies worry about a thing. That sculpture will be approved."

"Let's hope so," April said. "Now about Saturday night's meeting when the sculptor will speak to the townspeople. I thought the beautification committee might act as hostesses and provide some punch and cookies. Volunteers?" April quickly organized refreshments and cleanup for Saturday, and after some discussion about ordering seeds for next spring's planting on the square, the meeting was dismissed.

On the way out of the library Ida Mae touched April's arm. "Any chance Dan will change his mind and vote for the project?"

April shook her head.

"Too bad." Ida Mae glanced at April. "That's some coercive method of Mabel's."

"Uh-huh."

Ida Mae lowered her voice. "I guess she knows what she's doing, but I wouldn't try that on Dan if I were you."

April stopped walking and stared at her friend. "What makes you think I'd have the opportunity?"

"What makes you think I don't suspect what's going on?"

April smiled sheepishly. "And here I thought I was rivaling Irene's ability to keep secrets."

"I've known you too long, girl. Irene wouldn't have been able to keep secrets from her third-grade pal, either. She was lucky not to have one around."

"No, I think she was unlucky not to have someone like you, Idie. You've been terrific through all of this. I just don't want the whole town to know about Dan and me because we *are* on this board together, and people might think that wasn't proper, two board members—"

"In love?"

"I . . . yes."

"That's wonderful."

"But, Idie, this sculpture thing isn't making our relationship any easier. Sometimes when we argue about that, I feel as if he's the same old Dan, and I should stay far, far away from him."

"He's not the same old Dan, not from what Bill's told me. And because I'm your best friend, I'm going to give you some unasked-for advice."

"Which is?"

"Don't let this crazy sculpture ruin what could be the best thing that ever happened to you."

TRUE TO HER PROMISE in Chicago, April provided Erica with free lodging at the farm when she came to Booneville on Saturday. That meant Dan had to find a place to stay the night elsewhere, but under the circumstances of April's high visibility these days she thought it wiser, anyway.

Erica arrived late Saturday afternoon in a white Firebird that jolted noisily along April's lane and screeched to a stop in a cloud of dust. Through the car window April could see that Erica wore a red bandanna tied like a headband around her blond hair and an elaborately embroidered denim jacket. April decided this must be Erica's idea of country dress.

"You found the place," April said when Erica turned off the engine.

"Of course I did. Even drove through Booneville. It's a lovely little town, but it definitely needs a creative kick in the rear." She climbed out of the car and glanced around, her gaze lingering on the multicolored henhouse. "Nice place."

April glanced at Erica's skintight designer jeans. More of the sculptor's "country look", April decided. "It's quiet."

"True, except for the music. Why are you playing Beethoven out here?"

"The chickens seem to like it better than Bach."

"Oh." Erica gave April a strange look. "Of course."

April laughed. "A lot of farmers play music for their livestock these days. Experiments have shown that it calms the animals and makes them more productive. I've introduced my chickens to classical music instead of popular, that's all. So you see, I'm not as peculiar as you think."

"Shucks. I was hoping you were a certified loony, like me. And all the farmers paint their outbuildings rainbow colors for some scientific reason, too?"

"Okay, you've got me there."

"Aha! You are a fellow eccentric, even if you haven't learned to dress the part."

April laughed and glanced down at her wool slacks and sweater in neutral shades. "I have to make a few concessions if I want to live in Booneville."

"I understand. Think I'll get away with this garb? After all, they expect some weirdness, don't they?"

"I guess so," April admitted with a rueful smile.

"I'm counting on it. I've been giving this town a lot of thought recently."

"Have you brought some preliminary ideas to show people tonight?"

"Have I ever." Erica strode around to the trunk and inserted the key in the lock.

April followed her and caught sight of the rear bumper for the first time. "That's a rental sticker, Erica. Isn't this your car?"

"Nope. Don't have one. My studio's in my flat, and I take a cab everywhere else."

"Listen, Erica, I didn't realize you'd have to rent a car to come down here."

"Ah, don't worry about it." Erica waved a gloved hand. "I had fun getting behind the wheel again. Unfortunately the officer who stopped me didn't agree that I should have that kind of fun, but what's a little speeding ticket?"

April groaned.

"Anyway, here's my presentation for tonight." Erica gestured toward the boxes in the open trunk. "We're giving them a slide show. I already had pictures of my other work, and I had slides made of the preliminary sketches for this one so that everyone can see them better."

"You've gone to a lot of trouble and expense, and I'm beginning to feel guilty. At this rate the job could become very costly, and I wonder if it's worth the effort for you."

"It is." Erica braced her booted feet and put both hands on her hips. She looked nearly ten feet tall. "We're fighting the good fight, April." She flung one hand in the air. "We're dreaming the impossible dream. I love it."

April grinned. "I'm glad you came down, then."

"Me, too. Besides, you were right about the possibility for media attention. I can't measure everything I create in terms of how much money I make. This could be a very important sculpture for me."

"I'm dying to know what you've come up with."

"You'll love it." Erica picked up a long cardboard tube. "If we've got some time, I'll show you the sketches before we leave for the meeting."

"We've got time. I finished the chores early, so all we have to do is get you settled upstairs and eat supper."

"Great." Erica grabbed her overnight bag and slung it over one shoulder. "I hope you've got some of those cookies for dessert."

"Better yet, I made pumpkin pie."

"With whipped cream?"

"Yep."

"I'm going to love the country." Erica pronounced as she slammed the trunk shut.

Later April sat and gazed at the sketches spread out on her kitchen table. "*Growing Season*," she murmured. "This is fantastic, Erica. I can feel all the excitement of spring with new crops poking out of the ground and all those hopeful beginnings."

"I wanted to design something that would relate to the people here, to what is most important in their lives."

"And you've done just that," April said, filled with admiration. "They've got to love this. I certainly do."

"Yes, but you were crazy about *Impulse*, and not everyone else in town is, from what you've said."

"Oh, but there's a world of difference between a sculpture called *Impulse* and one named *Growing Season*. People around here can't allow themselves to be guided by impulse all that much. Money is too tight and traditions too ingrained. But the growth of crops is something everyone in Booneville understands and takes pride in. You've made an inspired choice of subject."

"Let's hope so. And you made an inspired choice for our dinner?"

"Meat loaf?"

"I never get to have it in Chicago."

"And to think I originally figured you for a real gourmet."

"Nope. I love basic dishes, but I can't cook even basic stuff worth anything. With me in the kitchen, simple food becomes simply awful. I can see you're talented in that direction, though. Plus you seem to have a successful business here. You appear to be firmly rooted, and I'm a little jealous of that."

"When I was growing up on this farm, I swore never to spend my life in Booneville, but now that's exactly what I want most to do." April sighed. "At least I think it is."

Erica studied her across the kitchen table. "Meaning you also want to be with someone who happens to live in Chicago?"

"How did you know?"

"It doesn't take a genius. When Dan Butler called me about coming down here, he let something slip about being with you in Booneville last weekend, and I know you were staying in his apartment up there."

"I should warn you that he doesn't approve of the sculpture project, at least not with something modernistic like this."

"So I gathered when he didn't rave about my work on the telephone."

April sighed. "I want so much for him to support this idea and show that he's able to take a risk for a change."

Erica lifted an eyebrow. "Show who?"

"Me, I guess. I don't know, Erica. I'm afraid to commit myself to a man who's so damn cautious, who won't rock the boat once in a while."

"Is he a coward?"

"No," April said immediately, shocked at the sound of the word applied to Dan. "That's not the problem."

"Then maybe he doesn't believe this is a risk worth taking."

"But if he'd think more creatively, he would see that it is. If he can't use his imagination more, I wonder if he's really the man for me."

Erica glanced at her. "Only you would know that. I haven't found a man yet who agreed with me on everything."

"But this is so important, so *symbolic*, don't you think?"

"For you and me, perhaps, but maybe not for him. Maybe he has other symbols."

April thought of the ring hidden away in her dresser drawer. His attitude toward the ring had surprised her, she had to admit. Still, his other reactions remained typical. He wouldn't reconsider his old aversion to farming, even if it was a way for them to build a life together. As for the sculpture, he would certainly vote against it unless Erica's presentation somehow changed his mind. As April cleaned up the dishes and Erica went over her notes for the meeting, April prayed that tonight's program would make a favorable impression on Dan.

IF SHE CLOSED HER EYES, April could pretend that the crowded 4-H hall was empty. Only a rare rustle of clothing or a subdued cough indicated that Erica was speaking to approximately four hundred people, or most of the able-bodied adults in the Booneville area.

April knew most of them by name. On the far side of the room her parents sat with Ida Mae's parents, Ed and Bernice Higby, and the Lowdermilk family, which numbered eleven adults. April wondered what all these people who had known her for years thought of this ruckus over a sculpture.

April's job was handling the light switches, and a few moments earlier she'd flipped them all down for the beginning of the slide presentation. Erica was standing to one side of the screen giving a narrative as the carousel automatically projected a series of sculptures, some large works in public places and others small pieces in elegant private homes throughout Chicago.

April was glad for the dim light. The less the crowd focused on Erica and her outfit the better. When she'd first stepped to the microphone, a murmur had rippled through the crowd, and April had noticed several elbows nudging neighboring ribs.

Only part of the stir was caused by the fact that the sculptor was a woman. Her mode of dress and her height also prompted heads to turn and usually reserved townspeople to stare. In her boots Erica was taller than most of the men here. Even Dan stood only barely even with her when they had met just before the presentation began.

As the person in charge of the program, Dan sat at the end of the first row of folding chairs. He'd introduced Erica to the crowd with a smooth diplomacy that gave no indication of his feelings toward her work or its appropriateness to the Booneville square. April was forced to admire his concerted effort not to influence the town's reaction.

At last Erica reached the portion of her talk in which she showed slides of her preliminary drawings. In an animated manner she discussed her idea and announced the title of the work. "I imagine *Growing Season* as a symbol of all you stand for here in Booneville," she said.

For the first time murmurs could be heard from the crowd.

"In addition to its obvious reference to your chief industry in the area, the sculpture will also demonstrate that Booneville is interested in the idea of growth itself, of the positive evolution of its citizens, of expanding the vision of the town to include such a progressive work of art in the very heart of the community."

April began to clap before she realized what she was doing. Tentatively some others in the crowd followed suit as the carousel clicked once more and the screen was blank.

"Thank you for your time," Erica said above the smattering of applause. "If we can have the lights back up, I'll answer questions."

Hands shot up as soon as April flipped the wall switches and illuminated the large room.

"We have a lot of children who play on the square," one woman said. "Would this sculpture be dangerous to them?"

"Not if I consider that when I design the final structure," Erica responded. "We can take into account a certain amount of climbing and playing around the base, and create the higher portions so they can't be scaled. I've done that before for park sculptures in Chicago."

Hiram Perkins stood up. "If you want something to represent Booneville, why not put up a giant cornstalk and be done with it? I could weld that together myself and save us all some time and money." Laughter greeted his statement, and when Hiram sat down again, April noticed Henry Goodpasture on his left. Henry carried a large mortgage on Hiram's farm and no doubt had put Hiram up to that last remark. Mabel's subversive tactics must not be working very well, April decided.

Then, to April's surprise, Bill Lowdermilk got out of his chair. His ruddy face was redder than usual, and he wore a stiff new pair of jeans. He stuck his hands in his back pockets and surveyed the crowd. "I'd like to comment on what Hiram said because I thought the same sort of thing myself once. Only I planned to have my kids make the sculpture at school out of pipe cleaners and modeling clay." More laughter swept the room. "But I've changed my mind, especially after hearing Miss Jorgenson's speech. How many of you grow corn? I mean to sell, not just for the table or your own animals?"

At least thirty hands went up.

"That's not even a majority. We grow lots of things besides corn around here. Soybeans, for instance."

Several others murmured their assent.

"I know most of the folks here," Bill continued, "and what they're raising. Even the ones raising Cain." He paused while people chuckled and winked at each other. "Anyway, I think we need something that represents all of us, and proves, like Miss Jorgenson said, that we're a town dedicated to growing. We're progressive. That's all I have to say on the subject."

As Bill sat down, April restrained herself from running over and hugging him. She couldn't have said it better, and many of the younger farmers, who looked to Bill for leadership, were nodding in agreement.

"And I say we'll be the laughingstock of the state if we put up this crazy thing," Henry Goodpasture remarked, rising from his seat.

Cheers went up from Henry's section of the hall, followed by angry accusations from the people surrounding Bill. A few insults were traded, and some fists waved in the air.

As the argument threatened to throw the meeting into chaos, Dan strode to the microphone and called for order. He'd listened to the presentation and the ensuing discussion with a sense of despair. He'd hoped that somehow tonight's meeting would change his mind, give him a reason to support April's project.

Instead, he discovered that the sculptor had created some romantic nonsense about growing crops, of all things. Henry was right; Booneville would be the laughingstock of the state if the town spent money on some idyllic monument to farming when so many people were going bankrupt. April and her followers were living in a rosy dream world.

The crowd seemed equally divided on the issue. Henry's derision of the idea had influenced those who feared him to join his camp and those who disliked him to lean the other way. Bill Lowdermilk had gathered some support with his statement. Dan wondered if he'd be able to talk some sense into Bill this week, before the vote.

And April. If he thought about her much at all, he'd forget about sticking with his beliefs. Would she ever forgive him for voting against her next week?

He took a deep breath and spoke into the microphone. "I'm sure that all of us on the board appreciate your input. We have a better idea of what's proposed now, and what your reaction is to it. We'll vote next weekend, so in the meantime feel free to contact any of us with your comments and suggestions."

"What do you think, Dan?" someone called.

Dan winced. They weren't going to leave him alone. He hesitated and shook his head. "I'd rather not continue the discussion at this time."

"But we know Bill's opinion, and Henry's, and of course we know April wants it," someone else said. "You're kind of in charge here. Do you think we should put this thing up or not?"

Dan concluded from the man's deferential tone and the silence with which the crowd awaited an answer that his response could very well make a difference. He wondered why his opinion would hold this sort of weight. Maybe it was because he was Irene's grandson or because he now lived in Chicago and was therefore considered more sophisticated.

Whatever the reason, he had the power to tip the scales either way. And he didn't want it.

He looked toward the back of the room, and his gaze found April's. *Forgive me*, he begged silently. He saw a look of panic cross her features. Did she suspect his decision? "I think this particular sculpture would be a mistake," he said clearly.

April felt as if he'd just delivered a blow to her stomach. How could he do this? The blood rushed to her head and her ears began to ring, but she forced herself to listen as Dan continued.

"Ever since the idea of a sculpture was proposed, I've tried to be open-minded and consider whether it would be worthwhile. Now that I see what Miss Jorgenson would like to create here in Booneville, I'm certain it would be a waste of money."

M.G. stood up for the first time. "Why, Dan?" he asked mildly, although April could see the older man's hands clenching the brim of his felt hat. "I think Miss Jorgenson has come up with something that will mean a great deal to all of us."

"That's part of the problem, M.G. She romanticized farming in this sculpture. That might have been okay fifty years ago, but farming's in a lot of trouble these days. Many of you are in debt. I'd rather take this money and hand it to some family that's having a tough time paying the mortgage than spend it on a sculpture that builds false hopes about how easy it is to grow things for a living."

The entire crowd, including April, was stunned into silence by Dan's assessment. He'd turned the subject of Erica's sculpture against itself, and for a moment April had no answer for him.

"I believe Dan's said it all," Henry proclaimed, rising and spreading his arms wide, "and we may as well go home and not fritter away more time on this. We'll take the vote next week, as he said, but I know what the decision should be, and so do all of you."

As the crowd began to stir, removing coats from the backs of chairs and purses from under them, April snapped out of her stupor. "Hold it!" she called and hurried toward the microphone at the front of the room.

She didn't look at Dan. Her intense anger might distract her from what she wanted to say. She stood on tiptoe and spoke into the microphone. "I know times are difficult for many of us. That's the very reason we need this sculpture. If we give this money to a family or two, they'd be very grateful, but then what of the many others who could use the same help?"

She paused to take a breath. "This sculpture is for inspiration, to remind all of us why we live in the country, why we pursue this crazy way of life in spite of the incredible odds. Isn't that sort of inspiration worth more than money? Money can only help a few, but a work of art could stand for centuries and tell the world that we in Booneville still believe in a *Growing Season*."

"I believe in feeding my family," someone said, and a large number of people applauded.

"What about feeding your soul?" April demanded.

"First we have to keep body and soul together," responded someone else.

Tears threatened, and her contact lenses began to hurt. She damned the reason for wearing them—to impress Dan. Now, thanks to him, her project had lost most of the support it had gained in the last week and during Erica's presentation tonight. She could still count on M.G.'s vote, and Bill's, but Gerald Sloan and Henry wouldn't have to change their minds because of public pressure, and neither would Dan. Her shoulders slumped as she realized that she had lost.

She barely noticed that Dan reached over and snapped the off button on the microphone. As she turned away, he spoke to her.

"I'm sorry, April."

She looked into his blue eyes and took pleasure in the agony she saw there. "So am I." She wanted to hurt him. "Why don't you come by on your way out of town?"

Faint hope flickered in his expression. "I thought you had a guest."

"I do. I'd like to return your ring."

Pain flashed across his face. "April, don't do this."

"I'd mail it to you, but that would be taking unnecessary chances with such a valuable item. I know you wouldn't want me to take unnecessary chances with anything."

"The ring is yours now."

"I don't want it. It's broken."

"What?"

"You heard me. It isn't working anymore."

"I don't believe you."

"You will. If you'll excuse me, I have to find Bill and thank him for standing by me." She turned toward Erica. "All packed up?"

"Yep."

"Then as soon as I talk to Bill, we can leave."

Dan reached for the case containing the projector. "I'll help you carry that."

Erica moved quickly and snatched the case before Dan picked it up. "We'll manage, thanks." Ignoring Dan, she glanced at April. "I hope you have something to drink in that farmhouse of yours."

As April walked away with Erica, she spoke loud enough for Dan to hear. "I have some very good wine. An acquaintance recommended it to me."

THE FIRST THING APRIL DID when she got home that night was take out her contacts and replace them with her large round glasses. The second was to open a bottle of Dan's favorite wine and pour two goblets full while Erica built a fire in the fireplace. After April put a tape of Beethoven sonatas on the stereo, the two women sprawled on the flowered sofa and polished off the bottle of wine. When it failed to blunt their anger, they opened a second bottle. Halfway through it the edges of their outrage began to soften.

"So I got you down here for nothing," April said, pouring the wine into Erica's glass with the exaggerated care of someone who is slightly tipsy.

"Not for nothing," Erica said, holding her glass up to the light. "This is good wine."

April giggled. "Good wine, bad man."

"Is there a chance he'll show up here to get that ring you mentioned? Because if we finish this second bottle, I may lose all restraint and kick his behind around that rainbow henhouse of yours."

April shook her head. "He won't show up. I was wrong about him. He's a chicken." She giggled again. "That's funny. If he's a chicken, you should kick him *into* the henhouse."

"No, my dear, he is not a chicken, and you're getting blitzed."

"I hope so." She took another swallow. "Why isn't he a chicken?"

"Because he said what he thought, even if it ruined his love life."

"It sure as hell did," April muttered. "His love life is terminal. Okay, he's not a chicken. He's a turkey."

"That I would agree with."

"Erica, do you hear a rapping noise?"

"No."

April crawled over to the stereo and turned down the music. "Now do you?"

"Yeah. Woodpeckers?"

April lowered her voice to a whisper. "Maybe it's him."

"You think so?"

"Maybe. What'll I do?"

"You could leave him out there."

April brightened. "I sure could." Then she frowned. "But I want to get rid of that stupid ring." She got slowly to her feet.

"If you let him in, I will not be responsible for my actions."

"Erica," April said solemnly as she stood swaying over her new friend, "I do not want bloodshed in this house."

"Then you'd better talk to him outside."

"Right. I'll get the ring." April meandered unsteadily into her bedroom and poked through her dresser drawer. "There you are, you scoundrel," she mumbled, and headed back in the direction of the front door as the pounding grew louder. She flung open the door, and Dan almost rapped on her face. "Shh!" she ordered, her breath creating fog in the night air. "The chickens are asleep."

"April, I can't leave things like this between us. I have to talk to you."

"Not necessary. Here." She thrust the ring at him.

"No. I won't take it." He peered at her. "Are you drunk?"

"Yes, and I want to stay that way. So I must get out of the cold. Here." She shook the ring at him. "Jus' take it and leave."

"April, I love you."

"Ha."

"Okay, so you won't believe me now, but keep the ring. Just—" He reached for her, and she stepped back a pace. "April, won't you let me—"

"No. Will you take this damn ring?"

"No."

"Then I guess I'll sell it."

"Sell the ring?" He stared at her in confusion.

"Sure, why not? What good is it on someone's finger, looking pretty? Why not have money, instead? That's Daniel Butler's philosophy."

His blue gaze grew anguished. "April, that's not what I—"

"It sure is," she said, trying to focus better. "He doesn't unnerstan' that people need beauty in their lives. We couldn't make it together, Dan and me." She laid the ring on the arm of the wooden porch chair. "If I fin' this here in the morning, so help me I'll sell it." Then she stepped inside and slammed the door.

BEFORE DAWN the next morning, her head aching from the wine consumed the night before, April climbed wearily out of bed. She had chores to do, but first she had to check the front porch. She remembered vaguely leaving the ring out there and telling Dan that if he didn't take it, she'd sell it. He'd probably left the ring, but of course she wouldn't sell such a beautiful heirloom.

If he had indeed left the ring, it would be a continued link between them, and April admitted reluctantly to herself that she still craved that link, in spite of everything. He was wrong for her; that much had been proved the night before. Unfortunately the knowledge hadn't changed her love for him. If she still had the ring, communication between then couldn't be permanently over.

A rooster crowed as she opened the door to the cold stillness of early morning and flipped on the light. The pale glow illuminated the arm of the old wooden chair. The ring was gone.

# 13

"I'VE SCREWED THINGS UP beyond belief." Dan hunched over the coffee mug Ida Mae placed in front of him and let the steam soothe his unshaven face. He felt physically and mentally ravaged by the hours of soul-searching he'd just been through, and finally he could think of no place to go but the Lowdermilks' warm kitchen.

"I wish I could tell you different," Bill said, accepting another cup of coffee from his wife. "But your statement at the end of the presentation last night changed a lot of people's minds. They won't be swayed back easily."

The ring in his slacks pocket dug against Dan's thigh as he shifted his weight in the kitchen chair. "I feel as if I've personally robbed Booneville of its chance to lay claim to something really special, something that would last through the generations. Why couldn't I have realized that sooner?"

"Your position wasn't wrong, Dan," Ida Mae said gently as she joined them at the round oak table. When Dan had arrived a half hour ago looking as if he'd been run over by a truck, Ida Mae had sent her children to a neighbor's house to play for the afternoon. Dan obviously needed uninterrupted help. "You had me half-convinced myself. Farmers *are* in trouble all over the county, and we would be spending money on something no one could eat or wear or use to pay the mortgage."

"Yes, but does anybody mention that when we talk about Mount Rushmore or the *Statue of Liberty*?"

Ida Mae smiled. "No doubt some people have, Dan, over the years."

"I don't want to be one of them," Dan grumbled. "My mother and father struggled with their farm, and she faced hard financial times when he died, but she never once considered selling her ring, which was her private work of art. I grew up knowing there were some things more important than hard cash. Why couldn't I make better use of that knowledge?"

Ida Mae patted his hand. "Sometimes we don't see the truths that are right in front of our faces. Don't be so hard on yourself."

"Okay, we'll forget about my stupidity. Now how can we have that sculpture for Booneville?"

"Oh, we can have it, all right," Bill said, sipping his coffee. "With your vote we'll win approval four to two. But the townspeople won't understand. Many of them will resent that sculpture after what was said last night. We might even have to worry about vandalism."

"We've got to get that support back, Bill. At this point April probably wants nothing to do with me, but I'd be glad to give her another chance to speak and then explain that my original assessment was wrong."

Ida Mae shook her head. "No good, Dan. People around here suspect that you're sweet on April. They'll think you've changed your mind because of her." Ida Mae couldn't help chuckling. "Especially considering Mabel's stand with Henry."

Dan frowned. "What do you mean, Mabel's stand?"

"Yeah, what do you mean, Idie?"

"You must both swear never to say I told you."

"Okay," they said together, both leaning forward in their curiosity.

"She's waging a bedroom campaign against Henry to get him to vote for the sculpture."

Dan and Bill looked at each other and began to laugh. Bill's face turned beet red, and Dan laughed until the tears rolled down his beard-stubbled cheeks.

"But," Bill said, gasping, "why do you suppose it isn't working?" He glanced at Dan and shook in silent mirth.

"I can't imagine," Dan said, and they both erupted into another fit of laughter.

Finally Dan dried his eyes and leaned his head in his hands. "I'm getting punchy after a night with no sleep."

"I thought you'd been up all night," Ida Mae scolded. "You were always the one who insisted on your eight hours."

"Yeah, April remembers that, too. Seems I have quite a reputation for being a stick-in-the-mud."

"You're conservative, Dan. That's no crime."

"I wonder. Anyway, I discovered last night that some things are more important than sleep, too, such as straightening out the mess I've caused." He glanced at Bill. "I think we've got to buy some time before the vote. Let's postpone it, for, say, three weeks. Maybe that will give me a chance to think of something."

"Henry won't like a postponement," Bill said. "But M.G. and Gerry Sloan shouldn't mind, and April won't care."

Dan looked across the table at Bill. "Will you call her and let her know? I— She might hang up on me."

"Sure. I'll handle the others, too. We'll get the extra three weeks, but I can't imagine how you can change anyone's mind in such a short time."

"Neither can I," Dan admitted. "Maybe I'll talk to Erica Jorgenson. She's mad at me, too, but somehow I feel safer approaching her."

Bill shook his head in dismay. "Sounds like choosing between a charging bull and a hornet's nest to me. That Erica is some tough lady."

Ida Mae surveyed the two men. "So is April," she said.

Dan considered her statement. He hadn't admitted to anyone how he felt about April, but the time for hiding feelings was over. "I guess that's a big reason why I love her," he said quietly.

THE FIRST HEAVY SNOWSTORM of the season arrived five days later and left April's farm looking as if it had been wrapped in cotton batting. Her father drove out to help her shovel a path to the henhouse and the beehives. She made certain the hive entrances weren't blocked with snow and double-checked the heaters in the henhouse. After years in the country she understood the importance of constant vigilance when the weather changed.

Usually she reveled in the simplicity of line that snow brought to the Illinois countryside. Often she'd snuggle in front of her cozy fire with a cup of hot chocolate and a good book, once she'd taken care of her routine chores, or she'd put chains on the old truck and drive over to Ida Mae's house where she'd help Idie's children build a snowwoman and a snowman.

But what she usually did wasn't applicable to her life these days. Once her necessary jobs were finished, she walked for hours along the icy country roads. She wasn't interested in company, but she loathed inactivity nearly as much, so she walked, staring at the fields extended along each side of the road like huge sheets of blank paper.

She was angry with herself for not being able to put Dan out of her mind. What did it matter that his touch set her on fire, if he had no sense of beauty in his soul? She ordered herself to stop loving this man who had smashed her dreams for the second time, but her rebellious heart wouldn't accept her command, and the ache for him went on.

The second day after the snowfall she returned to the farmhouse and was stomping the snow from her boots onto the front porch when the telephone rang in the kitchen. Each time she'd received a call in the days since Dan had left, she'd run to the phone with irrational haste, all the while telling herself that the caller couldn't be Dan.

This time she left her boots on as she hurried to the ringing telephone in spite of the wet tracks that would ruin her clean kitchen floor. She picked up the receiver and tried to control her rapid breathing.

"Hello?"

"Hi, sweetheart," her mother replied.

April stared dismally at puddles on the linoleum. "Hi, Mom. What's up?"

"Quite a bit, as a matter of fact. I think you'd better put the chains on the truck and take a drive into town. After you've seen it, you can come and have supper with us."

"Seen what?"

"I wouldn't dream of spoiling the surprise by telling you. Just make sure you drive past the square on your way over."

"Mom, I don't want to sound ungracious, but putting the chains on is a lot of work. Couldn't we have supper in a few days when the roads are clear?"

"Trust me, April, you'll want to see this. Put the chains on and come over, but drive past the square first."

"It had better be good, whatever it is. And remember I've seen the twelve-foot snowman that the Compton kids built last year. I don't want to go to all this trouble for something like that."

"Just do it, dear. You won't be sorry."

"Okay." April sighed. "See you in about an hour, after I've taken care of the chickens and put on the chains. This had better be good," she said again.

"It is," her mother promised, and hung up.

April suspected her mother of some sort of ruse to snap her daughter out of the doldrums. The whole town knew that April's sculpture project was in trouble, and many also suspected that her rumored romance with Dan had been sidetracked, too.

As April finished her chores and took the snow chains out of an old cardboard box, she tried to imagine what could be on the square that her mother thought worth seeing. If the gazebo had toppled under the weight of the snow, or one of the stately elms had fallen over, her mother wouldn't have sounded so cheerful and so . . . was excited the word? Yes, April decided, her mother's tone had been definitely excited.

April drove slowly, allowing the chains time to bite into the ice-encrusted road. She was the only one chugging along that afternoon, as lowering clouds brought an early twilight to the silent white fields. A lone cardinal, a splash of red in the nearly colorless world, perched on a snowy bush beside the road. April felt the pang of sadness that always came when she experienced beauty alone. Lovely sights weren't nearly as lovely without someone to share them.

Closer to town the traffic increased. Headlights were turned on against the gathering dusk, and the ice on the road sparkled. April thought, as she always did with the first snowstorm, of Christmas. Before the fateful night of the slide presentation she'd looked forward to the holiday and fantasized how she would spend it with Dan. Now she dreaded the enforced gaiety of the season.

A glow seemed to come from the direction of the square, and April increased the truck's speed a little. Whatever was there that her mother wanted her to see required light. April was becoming curious in spite of her best efforts to expect nothing more than another large snowman erected by the Compton boys.

As she rounded the corner next to Jesse's Café, April gasped. The snow-covered square was completely illuminated with several spotlights, and children scampered everywhere. At the center of the activity, on the corner opposite the gazebo, were two large scaffolds beside a tall ice-and-snow object that made April squint in disbelief. She must be imagining things, she told herself. But no, she'd studied those preliminary drawings carefully. Someone was building an ice-sculpture replica of *Growing Season*.

April parked the truck and hurried toward the square. A figure stood on the scaffold putting the finishing touches on the top while children sent more snow up in buckets attached to ropes and pulleys. A man directed the children, and as April approached, she recognized Bill under a knit cap and heavy winter jacket.

The person on the scaffolding wore a lavender ski jacket and matching pants, and even before April saw the blond hair tucked under the jacket's collar, she knew the person had to be Erica.

April walked up to Bill and tapped him on the shoulder. "What in the world is going on?" she asked when he turned around.

He grinned and gestured toward the ice sculpture. "Like it?"

April looked at him with a dazed expression. "I don't understand."

"We're going to have our sculpture, April."

"But this will melt."

"That's the idea."

"Bill, you're not making a lick of sense."

A shout came from above them. "Bill! I need another bucket of snow! Is that you, April?"

"Erica, what are you doing up there? I'm getting nothing out of Bill except double-talk."

"What I want out of him is another bucket of snow," Erica called back. "You two can talk later. I want to finish this so I can sit in front of a nice warm fire. You did promise that, right, Bill?"

"That plus a home-cooked meal and dessert," Bill called back as he motioned one of the children to dump snow in the bucket beside him.

When the bucket was on its way up to Erica, April grabbed Bill's arm. "Okay, let's have it. Otherwise, I'm having you two placed in warm padded cells for the winter. Why would you go to all this work for something that will be gone in a week or less?"

"Simple. We figure that if we show people how beautiful the sculpture will be, they'll come to accept the idea— like it, even. Then when the thing melts, they'll want it back in a more permanent version."

"But we'll have a tie vote on the board."

"Don't count on that."

"Really? You mean Gerry Sloan might change his mind? He's the only one I can imagine doing that."

"Maybe Gerry will change his mind, but I don't expect a tie."

"This demonstration won't change Henry's mind, and Dan is in Chicago and won't even see it, so I think you're working hard for nothing, Bill."

"Maybe."

"Was this your idea or Erica's?"

"I, ah, well, it was—"

"I bet you thought of it, Bill, you crazy, lovable man. Is Erica staying at your house, then?"

"Yeah. We wanted to surprise you, so we snuck her into town."

"Fat chance of that. I'm astounded no one told me until my mother called this afternoon."

"I'm sure a few people tried to tip you off, but it seems you haven't been home much lately to answer the phone."

"That's true," April admitted, thinking of her long, lonely walks. "Anyway, this is fantastic, even if it doesn't work. Can I do anything to help?"

"I think we're about finished, and the kids have loved every minute of it. That was part of the plan, to have the kids help after school so they'd feel a part of the project. I think they'll go home and beg their parents to ask for a permanent sculpture just like this."

April smiled. "They might. They might at that. You may turn out to be a genius, Bill."

"Don't give me all the credit."

"Okay." April called up to the woman on the scaffold. "You're terrific, too, Erica."

"Thanks!"

April turned to Bill. "I'm supposed to have dinner at Mom's, but why don't I come by later? I'd love a chance to talk to all of you."

Bill averted his eyes. "Um, I don't know, April. We'll probably be pretty tired after all this work. I think we'll turn in early."

"Oh. Okay." April tried to hide her disappointment. For some reason they didn't want her to be part of all of this. Yet hadn't the sculpture been her idea in the first place? She felt snubbed. "Guess I'll get on over to Mom's, then."

"Yeah. See you, April."

WITHIN AN HOUR Bill was at home talking long-distance to Chicago. "Why can't I tell her you were behind the whole thing? I'm having a damn hard time keeping it to myself, old buddy. She wanted to stop by this evening, and I had to be rude and tell her not to because I was afraid someone around here would spill the beans. Now she thinks we're shutting her out."

"I won't parade my virtues in front of her like some proud rooster, Bill. Maybe later, after the vote, we can discuss it, but not now. Do you think the plan will work?"

"I don't see why not. Everyone in town is buzzing with news of the sculpture and how beautiful it is. The kids will influence their parents, too. That was a real brainstorm on your part. Damn, I wish I could tell April."

"Please don't, Bill."

"Then I'll have to avoid her like the plague until we vote in two weeks."

"That's okay. The most important thing is getting the town behind the sculpture and then taking a vote, which should come out four-two in favor."

"I hope these two weeks go fast. And stay cold."

"Me, too. And take a picture for me, will you? I'll never know how it looked otherwise."

"You could come down next weekend."

"No, I couldn't. If I got that close to April, I'd probably go break her door down just to hold her in my arms. Let's get this sculpture business settled first."

"Okay, Dan. We'll do things your way."

"Thanks, buddy."

APRIL FOUND AN EXCUSE to go into town every day until the sculpture began to melt, and then she avoided driving past the square because the sight was so disheartening. She heard fragments of town gossip and realized that support for the sculpture had grown considerably, but what difference would that make if the board had a tie vote?

At the regular meeting of the Beautify Booneville committee April quizzed Mabel Goodpasture and concluded that Henry had not changed his mind, ice sculpture or no ice sculpture. That left Gerald Sloan. Finally, desperate to know if the project had a chance of success, she called him.

"Why, April, what a nice surprise," he said when she identified herself. "I haven't seen much of you lately. I thought you were mad at me because of the sculpture thing."

"No, not really," April said, knowing that she didn't harbor the same antagonistic feelings toward Gerry that she did toward Henry—perhaps because Gerry wasn't as pompous about his conservative opinions and didn't try to run the whole town single-handedly. "But I was curious as to how you felt, now that you've had a chance to see how the sculpture would look on the square."

"That was an interesting experiment, wasn't it?"

"Yes, it was." April held her breath.

"The sculpture looked better than I thought it would."

"I'm glad. Does that mean you've, um, altered your opinion?"

"Well, April, I'll tell you. I did give some thought to changing my mind because the sculpture looked so pretty, especially with the sun on the ice. It reminded me of cut crystal, you know?"

"I know."

"But I thought of all that money and decided that Henry is still right. We ought to look at the practical side of things."

April bit her lip to stifle a groan.

"I hope we can still be friends, April."

"Of course," she heard herself say. "I was just wondering if you'd changed your mind. I'll see you on Saturday for the vote."

April stared at the telephone after she hung up. Bill had made a noble effort all in vain. The vote would still be tied, and April couldn't imagine any of the board members budging. Booneville would lose its entire legacy from Irene unless . . .

April slumped in her chair. She only had one course of action open to her, and it made her furious to think of having to take it. After the voting was completed, she was resigning from the board. She never wanted to see Dan Butler again.

THE IVORY BEAUTY of the snow was tarnished with car exhaust and mud by the time Saturday arrived. April no longer needed chains to drive into town, and the place where the ice sculpture had once stood was a sloppy mess of ice and mud.

Jesse had agreed to close her café once again for a half hour, and people were gathered all around the square to await the outcome of the vote that would take place inside Jesse's establishment. April walked in with her glasses on and her jaw set. This would not be a pleasant morning, and she refused to smile at anyone, least of all the dark-haired man at the end of the table.

"I guess we're all here now," Dan said gruffly. "And we all know what this vote is about. So let's just go around the table and see what we've got. Bill?"

"I vote for the sculpture."

"Gerry?"

"I'm afraid I have to keep my original stance and vote against it, Dan."

"I understand. Henry?"

"You know good and well how I'm voting."

"Okay. April?"

Somewhere she found the strength to look him right in the eye. "I'm abstaining from the vote."

Dan appeared confused. "Abstaining? Why?"

"Because I can't bring myself to vote against the project, and yet we must avoid a tie. I don't recall anything in Irene's stipulations that covered abstaining, so that's the choice I've made. This way you won't have a stalemate, which could cause Booneville to lose everything."

A murmur of surprise went around the table. Bill opened his mouth to protest April's decision, but Dan shook his head and Bill remained silent.

"That's an admirable stand, April," Dan said, a hint of a smile on his lips.

She saw the smile and glared at him. "I thought you'd be happy with it."

His smile grew broader. "Let's finish the vote. M.G.?"

"I'll go down with the ship. I vote in favor."

Dan nodded. "So we have two in favor and two against and one abstaining."

"Get it over with, Dan," April muttered, staring at the Formica-topped table in front of her.

"Okay. I vote in favor. I guess the sculpture is approved."

April's head snapped up. "Pardon me?"

Henry stood up quickly, and his chair clattered to the floor. "You don't know what you're saying, Daniel. Let's talk this over, have another vote. Look, April even backed away from her own project."

"Only because she was considering the good of the whole town," Dan said quietly. "I wonder if you're doing that, Henry?"

April continued to gaze in bafflement at Dan. "You're voting in favor of the sculpture? But you said—"

"I was wrong. Unfortunately I didn't learn that until after the slide presentation. The damage had been done by then."

Bill cleared his throat. "But you fixed it, Dan. I think April should know that erecting the ice sculpture was entirely your idea."

April looked from Dan to Bill and back to Dan again. "It was?"

Dan shrugged. "I had to come up with some way to show the town how great the sculpture would look. Bill and I even thought of papier-mâché."

"What a mess that would have been," Bill said, shaking his head. "Luckily it snowed before this guy rounded up enough newspaper and paste, and he came up with the brilliant idea of creating the sculpture in ice, like those fancy restaurants do in Chicago. He finally talked Erica into giving it a shot, and here we are."

M.G. beamed at all of them, even the irate Henry. "I couldn't be happier, unless, of course, Irene were here to witness all of this."

"I think she's here in spirit," April said softly, gazing at Dan.

"Well, I won't be a sore loser," Gerry said, extending his hand across the table toward April. "Congratulations."

"I think you're all crazy," Henry said, and stomped out of the café.

Bill watched him go and chuckled. "If he plays his cards right, he'll go home and tell Mabel that he broke down and voted for the sculpture."

Dan grinned. "Maybe he likes things the way they are, Bill." The two men exchanged an amused glance.

"I hate to break this up," Jesse said, appearing from the kitchen, "but if what I overheard is correct, you've completed your business, and I've got a horde of customers waiting to come in and buy my coffee and hear my news."

"Sure, Jesse," Dan said, standing. "Let them in."

"I've got a pile of work to do at home," Bill said, heading for the door. "Congratulations, April."

M.G. and Gerry said their goodbyes and left just as the first of the townspeople entered the café.

"Let's get out of here," Dan mumbled and took April's elbow.

"Say, Dan," called one man in overalls. "How'd the vote go?"

"Jesse has the whole story," Dan said, and propelled April out the door.

"Dan," she said as they walked away from the crowd toward his car, "I have a few things I'd—"

"Good. Do you have some free time right now?"

"I . . . I suppose."

"Then let's go." He opened the passenger door of the red Honda and had her inside before she realized what was happening.

"Dan, where are we going?"

"You'll see. I hope there's still enough snow outside of town."

"Enough snow for what?"

He glanced at her and smiled. "To show you the new Dan Butler."

"The old one was pretty nice, except for a few unmentionable moments."

"Don't remind me. I'd made some progress, but not enough to count until recently. Thank God you suggested selling the ring."

"Dan! You didn't!"

He arched an eyebrow at her vehemence. "What if I have? Will you disown me again?"

"I . . ." She paused. "I never disowned you," she said, only now understanding that it was true. "No matter what you've done, I haven't been able to stop caring for you."

He reached for her hand. "That's nice to hear."

"But, Dan, that ring . . . it means so much to—"

"You?"

She fell silent, unwilling to admit how much the ring had come to symbolize their love for each other. If it was gone, she would still love him, but some of the magic would be lost.

"Never mind about the ring." Dan turned down a rutted lane toward an old farmhouse. "We have some other business to take care of."

# 14

"WHAT ARE WE DOING at the Tennerly place?" April asked as the Honda jounced along the road toward the farm buildings.

"You'll see."

"I can't imagine what you're up to, Dan."

"That's exactly the way I want it. Old Dan has been predictable long enough."

He stopped the car next to Will Tennerly's weathered barn. "Wait here. I'll be right back," he directed, leaving her in the car while he navigated through the ice and mud to the barn door. At his approach Will poked his crinkled face around the heavy door, and Dan followed him inside.

April sat in the car with an unsettled feeling she'd never experienced in connection with Dan Butler. She hadn't the foggiest notion what he'd do next. She was still digesting the information that he'd engineered the creation of the ice sculpture on the square, and that ever since her declaration about selling the ring, he'd planned to vote for the sculpture when the time came.

Had he really sold the ring? She couldn't believe that he'd do it, yet she wasn't prepared to predict what he'd do anymore. He'd always been exciting to her sexually, but now he was exciting her imagination, as well. The feeling was unfamiliar, but she was learning to like it.

Will Tennerly appeared at the barn door once more and laboriously pushed it back. April waited with anticipation. Whatever Dan had planned was about to happen.

First she heard the sound of bells, and then Will's swaybacked plow horse, Ned, who'd been out to pasture for at least five years, plodded out of the barn pulling a sleigh. April grinned at the sight of Ned, looking better than ever in his life, his mane and tail braided with red ribbon and brass bells jingling from his harness.

Dan jumped down from the sleigh to help her out of the car, but April had already opened the door and was crunching across the half-frozen ground toward him. "A one-horse open sleigh!" She laughed with delight. "I didn't know anyone around here still had sleighs."

Will Tennerly drew himself up proudly. "Mine's the only one in the county."

April smiled at him. "Ned looks wonderful, Mr. Tennerly. You've put a lot of work into this."

"You can thank Daniel, here. He made all the arrangements. Course, I did think of the ribbons myself, and the missus provided that lap robe."

Dan reached out and shook the old man's hand. "I appreciate everything you've done, Mr. Tennerly. You still think the back pasture has enough snow to make this thing work?"

"I'd expect so. Just go through that gate yonder and head east until you get to the creek. Then turn around and head back. Should give you a nice ride."

"We'll do that," Dan said. He turned to April. "Are you game?"

"Of course. I've never had a sleigh ride before."

"I was counting on that." He held out his hand to steady her while she climbed into the sleigh. "Especially since the tractor idea's a little shopworn."

She gazed into eyes as clear as the winter-blue sky above them. There was no doubting his purpose with this ride. "It is, isn't it?"

Her heart beat faster at the prospect of what Dan might say to her when they were alone. She wanted this man, wanted him more than almost anything else in the world. What would he ask her to give up for them to be together? How could he take her on a romantic trip through the countryside she loved and ask her to leave it for the city? Dan had made changes in his life, it was true, but April couldn't imagine that he'd decided to become a farmer after all.

As she snuggled under the red plaid lap robe, her feet bumped a paper sack that clinked with the impact. She glanced questioningly at Dan as he swung up beside her. "What have you got on the floor of this contraption?"

"Just ignore it," Dan said with a wink. "You're damn hard to surprise, you know that? Always asking questions." He picked up the reins and clucked to the horse.

"Okay." She'd already figured out that he had his favorite wine and glasses in the bag. His plan must be to take her out to the snowy seclusion of a deserted field and offer to toast their engagement. She loved the plan; she doubted the outcome. Many questions were still unanswered.

They waved to Will Tennerly as they drove out his back gate and into the pasture. The snow was a little thin, and the sleigh scratched more than glided across the ground, but April didn't care. The smoke from the Tennerly's fireplace drifted after them, and Ned's bells jingled cheerfully as he trotted with considerable spirit, considering his advanced age. April pretended she was in a scene from *Dr. Zhivago*.

As Dan shifted the reins to one hand, he reached over to draw her near. "Having fun?"

"You know I am. You're full of surprises these days, Daniel Butler."

He smiled at her. "That's the idea."

"The sculpture was beautiful."

"I know. Bill took pictures for me."

"It would have helped me to know that you planned that," she chided softly.

"I thought of telling you and trying to straighten things out between us earlier, but I changed my mind."

"Why?"

"I opted for the drama of having everything revealed at once. I decided that would appeal to you more."

"What?" April began to laugh. Had he grown to know her so well? "I guess you were right," she admitted sheepishly. "Damn, my glasses are fogging up."

"I figured Bill hadn't blown my cover when I saw those spectacles. You had no desire to impress me this morning."

"But I do now," she said softly.

"I've told you before, April, that you impress me with or without your glasses. I just don't like bumping into them when I kiss you."

"Are you planning to do that?" In spite of the cold she felt increasingly warm.

His arm tightened around her. "It's crossed my mind. We're almost out of sight of Tennerly's."

"Then I'll take them off. I wouldn't want to obstruct your— What's that noise?"

"Probably just the bottle and glasses on the floor. Never mind. Let's turn down here, closer to the creek. Then we'll have some privacy to . . . talk."

"Dan, I think something's wrong with the sleigh. Something may be coming loose underneath."

"Will Tennerly swore it was in fine shape the last time he drove it."

"Which might have been thirty years ago. Really, Dan, I think—" She was interrupted by a crunching noise, and the sleigh tilted to one side. "Dan!"

"Whoa, Ned, whoa!" Dan pulled back on the reins, and they both scrambled out of the sleigh. He peered underneath the crippled vehicle and swore softly. "The runner's come loose. Probably the bolts are rusted. I doubt if this damn thing will move another thirty feet, and we're well over a mile from the farm. What the hell are we supposed to do now?"

April began to laugh. "Is this the nostalgic version of running out of gas?"

Dan grimaced. "Hardly." He gazed in frustration at her smiling face and eventually began to chuckle. "Talk about typical. I try to be dashing and dramatic and the damn sleigh breaks. Next thing you know old Ned will fall down and die in his traces."

At the sound of his name the horse turned his head and looked at them with solemn tolerance in his big eyes.

"We can unhitch him and ride him back." April suggested.

"Let's unhitch him and tie him to that old stump so he can move around, but let's not go back. Not yet. I still . . . There's something that I want to—"

"We'll stay," April said gently, putting her hand on his arm. "I'm having a wonderful time, in spite of Will Tennerly's rickety sleigh breaking down."

"Me, too." As he gazed into her eyes, his frustrated expression was replaced with quickening desire. He squeezed her hand. "I'll unhitch Ned."

Within a few minutes they were seated in the sleigh once more with Dan on the lower side so that April slid naturally against his thigh when he helped her climb in.

"This has possibilities," he said, snuggling her against him.

"About that kiss . . ." She tilted her head and closed her eyes.

His mouth hovered over hers. "But first I think we should talk."

"Mmm."

"Hell. Forget that." He closed the gap between them and claimed the sweetness of her lips with a groan. She answered by opening to him and inviting a more sensual kiss, a stronger pledge of love and passion. He pulled her close and claimed the intimacy she offered, probing the inner recesses of her mouth and gauging the strength of her need by the tiny moan of pleasure that rose from deep in her throat.

With little conscious thought he fumbled with the zipper of her jacket and soon had his hand inside stroking her sweater-covered breast. Not until he found himself calculating whether he could make love to her on this tilted sleigh bench did he come partially to his senses.

"April," he gasped, lifting his head. Her lips were still partly open and red from the pressure of his mouth. Her eyes were closed.

"Don't stop," she murmured. "Love me, Dan."

"So help me I will," he promised fervently. "But not here. I brought you on this ride to talk out a few things."

Lazily her eyelids drifted open. "Could have fooled me."

"I always get like this around you."

She smiled with satisfaction. "No, you used to be much more controlled."

"That was before I knew what it feels like to slip inside you and love you until we both go crazy."

"Dan, I want you."

He took her hand and placed it against his groin. "I'm in the same shape," he said hoarsely. "But help me, April. We have to settle some things first."

She trembled as she felt his arousal and imagined how he could fill the aching void within her. "You're asking me to be the sensible one?"

His smile was lopsided. "One of us has to be, and I seem to be losing the job fast."

Slowly she withdrew her hand and put her head on his shoulder. Then she took a deep breath. "Okay, talk."

"Thank you." His hand shook as he rezipped her jacket. "This obsession I have scares me sometimes. I'm not used to being out of control."

"You don't like it?"

"That's the trouble. I *do* like it. I'm becoming addicted to the feeling of losing myself in you."

"That's not so bad."

"No. Not if you'll marry me."

She grew completely quiet. Here at last was the question that made the blood rush to her head and her hands tremble. Marriage to Dan. Lying beside him every night, waking to his kiss every morning. She ached for that life, but . . .

"Don't answer yet," he said softly. "That was only my opener."

"Quite an opener," she murmured.

"I wanted to start that way and let you know exactly how I felt, even though I probably have no business asking you to be my wife. Not yet, anyway."

She closed her eyes in fear. "Dan, please, don't start that. We had this conversation eight years ago."

"I know. Look at me, April." His blue eyes searched her face. "But I'm not the same man who held you eight years ago and explained why we couldn't get married. Did you hear what I said first of all? I want you to marry me, and to hell with the problems."

"I heard that, Dan. It gave me goose bumps."

He smiled. "Good. But now you have a right to hear the problems, anyway."

"I . . . I'll have to live in Chicago."

"Maybe not."

"Dan, you aren't considering farming?"

"No. I realize you'd want that, but I can't be happy as a farmer. I have to have something where more of my control comes into play. I may be able to give up command when I'm loving you, but not when my—our—livelihood is at stake."

"So what would you do?"

"Open a sporting-goods store on the square."

"Oh!" Impressed as she was with his idea, she knew better than to be overly enthusiastic. Booneville was a small town, and businesses didn't automatically survive there. "Of course that would be the perfect solution, but we both know there's a big risk involved."

"Yep. But I'd rather take that risk than put all of my resources into farming."

"Dan, I believe it will work," she said, excitement creeping into her voice in spite of herself. "There's the high school. I think they buy everything in Springfield now, but with you here that would change. More and more people are getting into fitness, even in Booneville. You'll make it, I just know you will."

"Maybe not, April. That's why you might want to wait and find out before you make any commitment to me. I have to make a living somewhere, and I hope it's in Booneville, but if not, I'll be forced to look elsewhere."

"It doesn't matter."

"What?"

She lifted her head to look directly into his eyes. "You heard me. The answer is yes, Dan. I'll marry you and gladly take that chance. You'll do your best to keep us in Booneville, and that's all I can ask."

Relief erased the tense lines on his face as he absorbed what she'd said. "April, I love you."

"And I love you."

They sat in the white silence and gazed at each other, each unwilling to spoil the moment with the inadequacy of words. A single bird chirped, and April wondered if it could be the cardinal she'd seen before. Now, at long last, she had Dan to share the beauty with her. For always.

He touched her cheek. "This is when we're supposed to drink a toast, but I'd rather go home and make love to you."

"And you went to all the trouble of bringing the bottle and glasses out here."

"Let's take them back. We can drink it later."

Desire quickened her tongue. "Yes, let's."

The journey to April's bedroom became a quest for solitude. After riding Ned back to the Tennerly farm, they quickly tried to extricate themselves from a long discussion of the sleigh's problems. Dan promised to come back the next day and help Will retrieve the vehicle.

Then they made a mad dash into town to pick up April's truck from the square and excused themselves from talking with several people sauntering along the sidewalk. Once away from town, they drove in tandem well over the speed limit to reach the seclusion of April's farm. When they arrived, she hung her Eggs Sold Out sign on the mailbox by the road.

Finally they stood in her bedroom holding each other and kissing as if they were survivors of a shipwreck.

"I thought we'd never make it," Dan said as he tried to kiss April and remove her clothes at the same time.

"First Tennerly and then all those people who stopped us on the square." She peeled off his shirt and kissed his chest. "Can we tolerate a small town, Dan?"

"They'll just have to learn," he replied, sliding her jeans over her hips, "that we require a certain amount of privacy."

She stepped out of the jeans. "A lot of privacy," she breathed as Dan reached beneath her panties and caressed the damp triangle concealed by white lace. "Oh, Dan." She undulated her hips against his probing fingers.

"Tons of privacy." He bent to kiss her gently swaying breasts.

"Come to bed," she murmured, drawing him toward the soft mattress as she worked at the fastening of his pants.

"I thought you'd never ask." He finished her undressing job and tumbled with her onto the bed. "Mmm, the sheets smell of you. Fresh as the country."

"I want them to smell of you." She pulled him on top of her. "That warm, sexy man-scent of yours." She rubbed her nose against his chest. "I love it."

"Tell me what else you love. This?" He kissed her deeply, taking her breath away before lifting his head and gazing down at her.

"Yes," she whispered.

"This?" He kissed her throat and gradually moved lower until he took her nipple in his mouth and sucked gently.

"Yes, oh, yes." She arched against him.

At last he spread her thighs and touched the throbbing spot with his manhood. His breathing was labored. "This?"

"Yes!" Gripping his hips, she urged him forward.

"April," he said into her ear, "I don't have any protection."

She looked up at him, her voice fierce with love. "I don't care. I want your children. Our children."

A look of primitive joy flared in his eyes. "So do I," he said hoarsely, and plunged into her.

ONLY ONCE THAT DAY, when Dan brought out the bottle of what turned out to be champagne instead of his favorite wine, did April think of the heirloom ring. Dan had not mentioned it again, even when he had proposed to her. She wondered if he had indeed sold it, and if not, where in the world it was.

At dinner that night, which Dan had arranged in a secluded corner of Jesse's Café, she found out. The meal had been interesting. Despite Dan's request for medium-rare steaks, Jesse had cooked them her usual way—fried to a crisp. There had been some trouble in the kitchen removing the cork from the wine bottle, and consequently the wine contained tiny bits of bobbing flotsam. In addition, Dan had forgotten to emphasize that baked potatoes usually accompanied filet mignon, not French fries.

The two lovers chuckled their way through the courses, held hands and stole a kiss whenever no one seemed to be looking.

"Honestly, it's the most romantic dinner I've ever had," April said, as Dan tried for the third time to light the candle stuck to a saucer in the middle of their table.

"I think the romantic part will have to come later, after we get back to your bedroom." Dan succeeded in lighting the candle and placed it away from the draft that had been snuffing it out all evening.

Jesse appeared beside their table. "Everything all right over here?"

"Just fine," April said, beaming at her.

"Are you ready for that other item, Dan?"

Dan glanced at April. "Anytime, Jesse."

"I'll be right back."

"Dan, you're doing it again."

"What?"

"Springing stuff on me."

"You bet. I'm really getting the hang of this business now. You'll never know what's coming next."

She smiled uncertainly. "I see."

"Hey, don't worry." He covered her hand with his. "Underneath I'm still the same steady guy. And there's one thing you can count on, no matter how many crazy stunts I pull. I love you, April. I always will."

"I'm so glad, because I need you desperately."

Jesse cleared her throat to alert them of her approach. "Well, here it is. Not exactly perfect, but you get the idea."

April stared at the object Jesse placed on their table.

"If you look at it from a certain angle, it does look like a heart," Jesse offered, cocking her head to one side.

Dan groaned. "What angle—standing on your head? I thought you said you could do an ice sculpture?"

"I thought I could," Jesse said. "It's harder than it looks."

"Oh, well." Dan glanced at April, who seemed to be mesmerized by the dripping chunk of ice. "We tried."

"The . . . the ring," April whispered. "You didn't sell it."

"Of course not," Dan said, taking her hand as Jesse tactfully retreated. "It belongs to you, to us. It's a symbol of the love we've found."

"I believe that, too." Tears sparkled in her eyes. "It really is a magic ring."

He shook his head and picked up the candle to melt the ice away from the brilliant piece of jewelry. "I'm not sure if the ring has special powers or if you do. Probably a little of both, but I know where this heirloom belongs." His hand trembled slightly as he picked the emerald-and-diamond ring out of the sculpture and slipped it on her finger.

April swallowed. "Dan, the stones seem brighter, more beautiful than before. You'll probably laugh at me for imagining such a thing is possible."

Dan held her hand and gazed into her eyes. "Never. With you in my life, everything has become possible."

"Even magic?"

His gentle smile was for her alone. "Especially magic."

# *Epilogue*

ONCE THEY DISCOVERED the impending wedding of Dan and April, the townspeople of Booneville expected no less than a June ceremony on the square followed by a hot-dog roast. The happy couple refused to wait that long, however, and eloped within a week after announcing their engagement.

As a compromise to the disappointed citizens, April and Dan promised a grand reception on the square during the last week in June, after Erica completed the sculpture. They even agreed to repeat their wedding vows and cut a cake fashioned by Jesse Hardcastle in the approximate shape of *Growing Season*.

From Christmas until June Dan worked hard to establish his sporting-goods store. Booneville and neighboring towns responded to his efforts, and business also increased for April at The Birds and the Bees. She joked with Dan that she might need some tutoring in the subject of birds and bees, however, because she still wasn't pregnant.

Dan concluded that they were both too distracted with work to make babies properly. He suggested taking a long-overdue honeymoon following the June ceremony so they could concentrate on the matter for an entire week.

Therefore April's glow of anticipation was genuine on that bright summer afternoon when she and Dan re-

affirmed their vows before the assembled residents of
Booneville. Her simple summery dress and wide-brimmed
straw hat reflected the carefree jubilation she felt at having her man all to herself for seven days.

The square had never looked more lovely, with beds of
petunias and pansies planted by the Beautify Booneville
committee surrounding the gazebo where the ceremony
was held. Across the expanse of lush grass, mowed the day
before expressly for the event, rose the graceful work of
art called *Growing Season*. Reporters and photographers
from as far away as Chicago and St. Louis clustered near
the shining flanks of the sculpture and awaited an opportunity to interview the attractive couple pledging their love
in the dappled shade of the gazebo.

Even Henry Goodpasture was in a mellow mood because the new sporting-goods store on the square was lo-
cated next to his bank, and he'd noticed an improvement
in his own business. He and Dan talked often, having
neighboring businesses, and one day Henry had mentioned all the travel brochures on European vacations that
were lying around his house these days.

Dan had asked to borrow a few. Before Henry could talk
them out of it, Dan and April had made reservations he
thought they could probably ill afford at a newly opened
luxury resort in France. Henry gazed up at the couple em-
bracing in the gazebo and shook his head. Dan was turning into a romantic fool if he thought there might be some
connection between a resort named Montclair and the
chicken scratching inside that emerald ring April wore.

As the lovers drew apart and smiled at each other, Mabel nudged Henry in the ribs. "They're so beautiful,
Henry."

"They're nuttier than fruitcakes, Mabel." Henry sighed and glanced over at the sculpture thrusting upward into the blue sky. "I don't get it. Dan Butler used to be such a sensible young man."

# ABANDON
# YOURSELF TO

*Temptation* ™

## TEMPTATION WILL BE
## EVEN HARDER TO RESIST...

In September, Temptation is presenting a sophisticated new face to the world. A fresh look that truly brings Harlequin's most intimate romances into focus.

What's more, all-time favorite authors Barbara Delinsky, Rita Clay Estrada, Jayne Ann Krentz and Vicki Lewis Thompson will join forces to help us celebrate. The result? A very special quartet of Temptations...

- **Four striking covers**
- **Four stellar authors**
- **Four sensual love stories**
- **Four spellbinding jewels**
- **THE MONTCLAIR EMERALDS...**
  **you'll be dazzled!**

TDESIGN - 2BR

The Montclair Emeralds . . . a priceless symbol of enduring love from a French nobleman to his lady. . . The jewels have traveled from seventeenth-century France, through time and circumstance, to four far-flung corners of twentieth-century America. To this day, they are still working their magic—a legacy of undying passion to the lovers who possess them. . . .

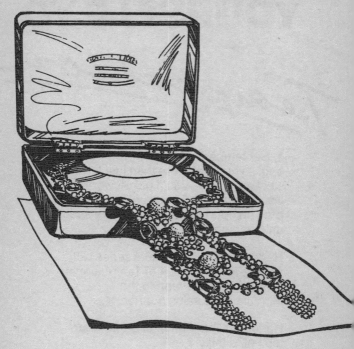